D1629508
APRIL -
brings the primrose sweet
Scatters daisies at our feet.
MAY -
brings flocks of pretty lambs,
Sporting round their fleecy dams.
JUNE -
brings tulips, lilies, roses,
Fills the children's hands with posies.

Catherine M. Muirden
12 Culcabock Road
Inverness
19th September
1971
Diana
for
FASHION
MYSTERY
BALLET
PONIES
ADVENTURE
FUN
POP
MAGIC
PETS
FILMS

Diana
for GIRLS

Printed and Published by
D. C. THOMSON & CO., LTD.,
DUNDEE and LONDON.

MY BIG BROTHER MARMADUKE

When the girls eventually left Duke alone, his pockets were bulging with notes!
LOOK AT YOU! YOU'RE LIKE A WALKING WASTE PAPER BASKET! THEY'LL ALL SAY THE SAME THING, I BET. 'TAKE ME TO THE DANCE, DUKE.' YUGH!

Even on the road home, Duke was not allowed to forget about the dance . . .
YOO-HOO, DUKE! JUST THOUGHT I'D TELL YOU, NO-ONE'S ASKED ME TO THE DANCE YET!
OH! OH, WELL, THANKS FOR TELLING ME, MONICA. I'LL KEEP YOU IN MIND.

YOU WILL, DUKE? HONEST? OH, WAIT UNTIL I TELL THE OTHER GIRLS!
WAIT A MINUTE, MONICA, I ONLY SAID—

THINGS ARE LOOKING BAD! I CAN SEE WE'RE NOT TO HAVE ANY PEACE AROUND HERE. THINK I'LL VOLUNTEER THAT DUKE AND I DECORATE THE HALL.

Word of Duke's 'volunteering' must have got around, for next day when we reached the hall—
OH NO, HOW DID THEY FIND OUT?
I THOUGHT I WAS TO COME HERE TO GET AWAY FROM THEM ALL?

The teacher in charge was just as amazed.
I CAN'T UNDERSTAND THIS SUDDEN BURST OF ENTHUSIASM! LAST YEAR WE HAD THREE VOLUNTEERS—THIS YEAR, WE HAVE FIFTY THREE!

Duke was detailed to hang the roof decorations.
I'LL HOLD THE LADDER STEADY, DUKE.
YOU MUSTN'T FALL AND HURT YOURSELF, DUKE—TAKE CARE.
NO, LET ME! I WAS HERE FIRST!
The girls fought and argued around the ladder until—
CELIA! YOU CLUMSY ELEPHANT! THAT WAS ALL YOUR SILLY FAULT!
AAGH!
The girls were so busy blaming each other, they forgot about Duke—hanging from the beams.
HELP! SOMEONE HELP!
Later, Duke and I left in disgust.
WELL, THAT PLAN WAS A REAL DISASTER! SORRY, ABOUT THAT, DUKE!
Next day at school, things were going from bad to worse . . .
I SAY, GIRLS, DO YOU THINK I MIGHT HAVE MY DESK?
IF YOU TELL US WHO YOU'RE TAKING TO THE DANCE.

That night at home.
JANE, WHERE ARE YOUR BRILLIANT PLANS? I CAN'T GET ANY PEACE! IT'S HOPELESS!
YOU CAN'T STAY IN AT NIGHTS, EITHER, BECAUSE MUM AND DAD OBJECT TO ALL THE GIRLS HANGING ABOUT THE FRONT GATE. YOU'LL HAVE TO FIND SOMEWHERE YOU CAN GO WHERE THEY WON'T FIND YOU. EITHER THAT, OR—

MAYBE THIS IS A BIT OVER-DRAMATIC, BUT HOW ABOUT IF YOU WERE TO DISGUISE YOURSELF?
ANYTHING! JUST SO LONG AS I GET THOSE SILLY GIRLS OFF MY BACK.

The next Saturday, when I was in town . . .
THE VERY THING! WE CAN DRESS DUKE UP AS SANTA, AND HIRE HIM OUT TO CHILDREN'S PARTIES!

At first, Duke wasn't too keen on the idea.
THIS BEARD WILL MAKE ME SNEEZE!
OH, DO STOP FUSSING, DUKE! YOU MUST BE PREPARED TO PUT UP WITH A LITTLE DISCOMFORT. IT'S IN A GOOD CAUSE!

Duke was a great success as Santa Claus.
LOVELY TOYS FOR US!

But helping out at one of the parties was a girl from our school . . .
AND NOW, CHILDREN, SANTA MUST JUMP ON HIS SLEDGE AND GET BACK HOME.
THOSE EYES, AND THAT VOICE—

Taking 'Santa' quite by surprise, the girl unmasked him.
I THOUGHT SO! DUKE!

Duke took to his heels.
LOOK, MUM! ISN'T SANTA A FAST RUNNER FOR SUCH AN OLD MAN!

Next day at school.
DUKE! I HARDLY RECOGNISED YOU ON YOUR OWN! WHERE ARE YOUR FANS?

I TOLD THEM THAT I'VE DECIDED WHO I'M TAKING TO THE DANCE.
YOU HAVE! WHO IS IT?

YOU'LL SEE!

On the night of the dance, the school hall was buzzing with excitement.

You can imagine the girls' faces when Duke walked in with—
HIS SISTER!
JANE!

Duke danced with me all the time, to save causing any trouble amongst his jealous fans.
WHAT A WASTE! THAT'S THE FOURTH DANCE HE'S HAD WITH JANE!

Half-way through the evening, however, there was a shattering announcement!
THE NEXT DANCE WILL BE A LADIES' CHOICE—

Talk about a stampede!
I BAGS THIS DANCE, DUKE.
DUKE, WILL YOU PLEASE DANCE WITH ME?
DON'T DANCE WITH HER, DUKE! DANCE WITH ME!

Poor Duke disappeared from view! Well, at least he'd got half the evening in peace.
YOU'RE STANDING ON MY DRESS, BARBARA.
STOP PUSHING! YOU'RE LIKE A PACK OF ANIMALS!

DUKE! DUKE! SPEAK TO ME!
OOF! LET ME OUT OF HERE!

After the dance, I had to take Duke home!
PHEW! I'M CERTAINLY GLAD I ASKED YOU TO THE DANCE, JANE. OTHER-WISE, I'D HAVE NO-ONE TO HELP ME HOME! OUCH, MY FEET, MY LEGS, MY HEAD—OOH!

Sketch-a-Star

Have you ever seen a caricature of your favourite star and wondered how it was done? Well, now's your chance to find out. Our artist has broken down drawings of Lulu and Bob Hope into easy stages for you to follow.

First, study a photo of the star. Then pick out his or her main features—in Lulu's case, a round face, big eyes and a flashing smile. And Bob Hope's famous nose and chin are obvious starting points. Exaggerate these features in your drawings, building them up step by step and rubbing out the rough lines when you are finished.

Have patience and you will be amazed at the results. Now try to spot the stars on the opposite page.

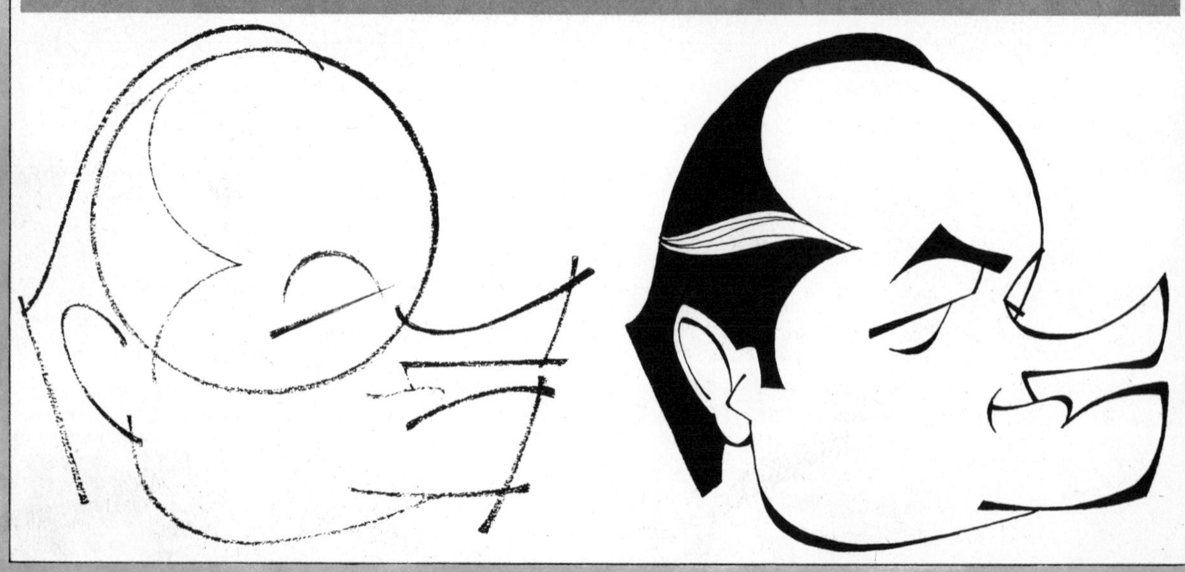

ANSWERS: George Best.
Ringo Starr. Jimmy Savile.
Mr Spock (from "Star Trek").
Dusty Springfield. Judith
Durham. Laurel and Hardy.
Marty Feldman. Ena Sharples
(Violet Carson). Paul Newman.

SARA and the SINGING PLANET
IT'S the year 2072, and through the vast blackness of outer space streaks a spaceship from Earth . . .
On board the ship were Professor Mitchelson, an interplanetary geologist, his wife, and his fourteen-year-old daughter, Sara.
HM! WE SEEM TO BE DRIFTING OFF COURSE. I'LL HAVE TO...
Suddenly—
LOOK, DAD! THAT PLANET. WHAT IS IT?
I'VE NO IDEA! WE MUST BE FURTHER OFF COURSE THAN I THOUGHT!
Just then the whole ship seemed to be filled with weird music, and strange, hypnotic shapes appeared on all the scanners.
LISTEN! IT SOUNDS AS IF THE PLANET IS SINGING!
THAT NOISE! AAAAH!
YES, I WILL LAND ON YOUR PLANET...
Sara and her mother slumped down, unconscious. The professor remained at the controls, but was in a kind of trance, moving like a robot.

Minutes later, the Mitchelson's spacecraft made a rough landing on the strange planet.
Dazed, but otherwise all right, Sara and her parents staggered out of the ship.
Then—
IT'S THAT STRANGE MUSIC AGAIN—BUT IT'S DIFFERENT THIS TIME. SWEETER SOMEHOW.
I'M GLAD YOU THINK SO. IT SOUNDS SINISTER TO ME.
With a great roar, a small vehicle appeared. In it were four young men.

The car screeched to a halt and the men jumped out.
THEM! OLDIES! TAKE THEM!

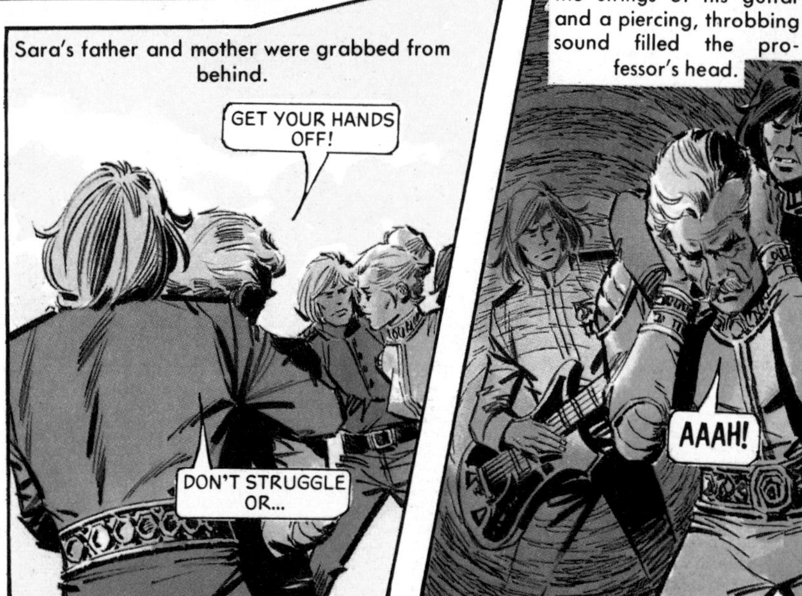

Sara's father and mother were grabbed from behind.
GET YOUR HANDS OFF!
DON'T STRUGGLE OR...
One of the men touched the strings of his guitar and a piercing, throbbing sound filled the professor's head.
AAAH!

Half-an-hour later, Sara was strolling through a large town. All over the place were huge posters of a young man with long silky hair. Every so often, announcements were made from hidden loudspeakers.

DON'T FORGET, KIDS! DEE JAY KNOWS WHAT'S GOOD FOR YOU! TRUST DEE JAY TO KEEP THE SCENE GOING!

I'LL ASK THIS GIRL.
HI! MY NAME'S SARA. I'D LIKE TO ASK...

The girl walked right past.
MUST GET THE KONKS' NEW RECORD...MUST GET...
OH, HERE YOU ARE!
The girl took Sara's record, and immediately came out of her trance-like stat e.
DO YOU KNOW WHERE THIS DEE JAY CHAP LIVES?
WHY, IN THAT BIG BUILDING BEHIND US. EVERYONE KNOWS THAT—BUT NO-ONE GETS IN.

DEE JAY HAS OBVIOUSLY BRAIN-WASHED ALL THE KIDS HERE WITH HIS WEIRD MUSIC AND WHAT-NOT. IT DOESN'T HAVE SUCH A STRONG EFFECT ON ME BECAUSE I DON'T HEAR IT EVERY DAY. STILL...

THAT GIRL SAID NO ONE GETS INTO THIS PLACE SO DEE JAY PROBABLY HAS A "MUSIC BARRIER" ROUND IT. I WON'T TAKE ANY CHANCES. THIS COTTON WOOL SHOULD DO THE TRICK!

Sara walked calmly into the building, and found, to her surprise, floor upon floor of empty rooms.
THE WHOLE PLACE SEEMS DESERTED. BUT THE GIRL SAID EVERYBODY KNEW DEE JAY LIVED HERE.

But, at last, on the top floor, found a room crammed with enormous machines, and sitting in front of them was—
DEE JAY, I PRESUME!

YOU'RE...YOU'RE OLD!
HEY! HOW...

COME HERE!
Sara flicked a switch on one of the machines.

The room filled with music.
LIKE MUSIC, DEE JAY? LET'S DANCE!
Sara danced about, evading Dee Jay's lunges.
Before long, Dee Jay was exhausted.
RIGHT! LET'S TONE DOWN SOME OF THIS MUSIC!

Soon, Sara's face appeared on TV screens all over the planet.
HELLO, KIDS! NOW'S YOUR CHANCE TO SEE DEE JAY AS HE REALLY IS!

Then Sara flashed Dee Jay's face on the screen.
WHY! HE'S OLD!
OLDER THAN ME OLD MUM, EVEN!
HE'S BEEN TELLING US A LOAD OF RUBBISH!

Soon the young people were rushing to the factories where their parents worked.
And they were re-united with their mothers and fathers. Thanks to Sara, the reign of Dee Jay and his hypnotic music was over.
MUM! MUM!

Not long after, Sara found her parents and soon the Mitchelsons' spacecraft took off.
On board—
THAT MUSIC! UGH!
NOT AGAIN!
IT'S ALL RIGHT. IT'S ONLY THE KONKS' LATEST RECORD. I THINK IT'S NOT BAD ACTUALLY!

UP-TO-DATE KATE

OUR DEDICATED FOLLOWER OF FASHION

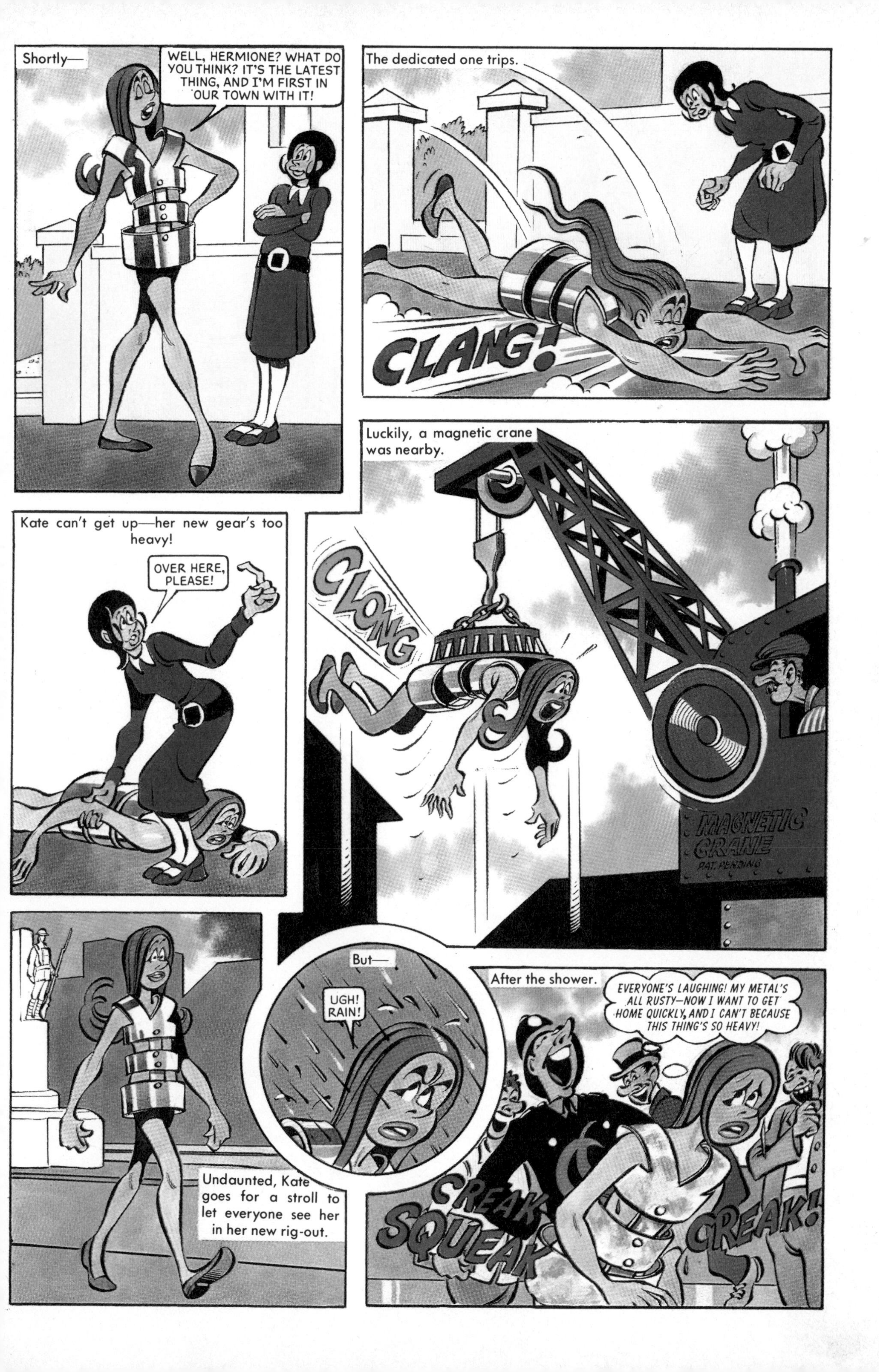
Shortly—
WELL, HERMIONE? WHAT DO YOU THINK? IT'S THE LATEST THING, AND I'M FIRST IN OUR TOWN WITH IT!
The dedicated one trips.
CLANG!
Luckily, a magnetic crane was nearby.
Kate can't get up—her new gear's too heavy!
OVER HERE, PLEASE!
CLONG
MAGNETIC CRANE
PAT. PENDING
But—
UGH! RAIN!
Undaunted, Kate goes for a stroll to let everyone see her in her new rig-out.
After the shower.
EVERYONE'S LAUGHING! MY METAL'S ALL RUSTY—NOW I WANT TO GET HOME QUICKLY, AND I CAN'T BECAUSE THIS THING'S SO HEAVY!
CREAK
SQUEAK
CREAK!

Get Packing!

For those who find packing for the summer holidays a chore and bore we've made up this list with you in mind. Happy travelling!

Useful dresses are ones which can be rinsed out and which drip dry. No ironing is necessary and they are usually cheaper to buy!

You'll need to take a nice bright sponge bag with you. There are plenty about in the shops to choose from!

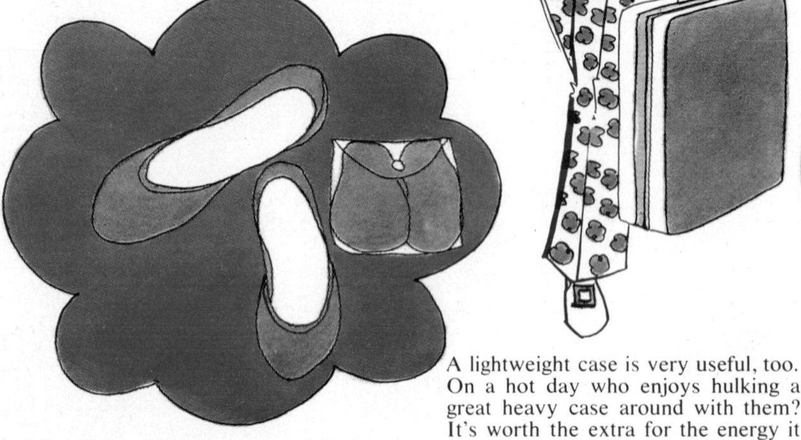

Plastic slippers fold away into their own pouch and cost very little. They're a must for the travelling Miss.

A lightweight case is very useful, too. On a hot day who enjoys hulking a great heavy case around with them? It's worth the extra for the energy it saves you.

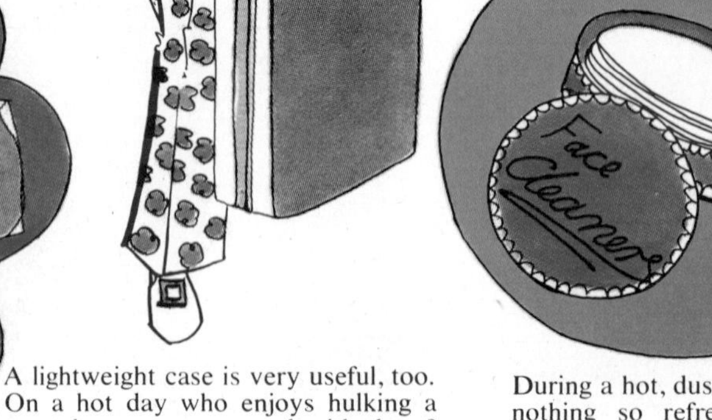

During a hot, dusty journey, there's nothing so refreshing as a face cleanser. You can buy a tin of these at any chemist.

'Barley sugar' sweets are useful when on air and train journeys and can often help anyone who feels queasy spend a more comfortable journey.

Make sure your handbag for travelling is large and bright. You'd be surprised at the amount that it will have to take.

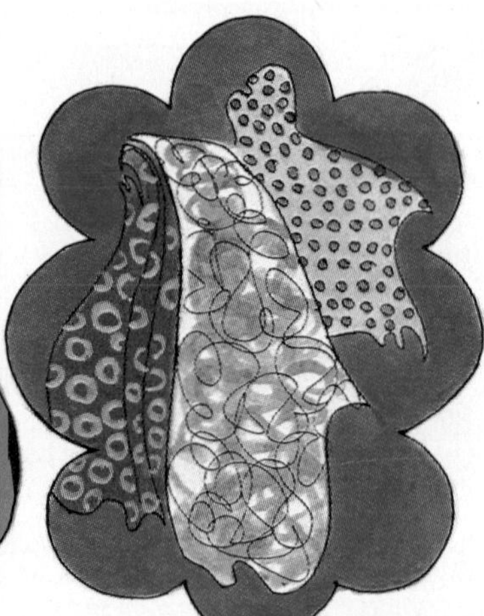

Remember – a selection of coloured scarves are helpful accessories to brighten up any holiday outfit.

JANE - Model Miss

YOUNG Jane Morgan is a fashion designer who owns a boutique. One day, when she and her models were preparing their latest creations . . .

When the stranger left . . .
HOW STRANGE. BUT I WON'T CHANGE MY MIND, NOT WITH A FREE TRIP ROUND THE WORLD TO LOOK FORWARD TO. IN FACT, THE SOONER I GET ON WITH THE UNIFORM...
A few weeks later—
HOW DO YOU LIKE THE UNIFORMS. MR WRIGHT?
THEY'RE VERY ATTRACTIVE, JANE. IF THEY WEAR AS WELL AS THEY LOOK, YOU'LL WIN A BIG ORDER FROM THE COMPANY.
THESE ARE THE PEOPLE YOU'LL HAVE TO IMPRESS, JANE, THE DIRECTORS OF AIR-WAYS TRAVEL AND THEIR FASHION ADVISERS.
Soon, the plane was soaring through the sky.
WELL, GIRLS, IT'S A FREE TRIP FOR YOU BUT YOU'LL HAVE TO WORK TO PUT THE UNIFORM THROUGH ITS PACES. LOOK, MR CARTIER, THE FASHION DESIGNER, IS TRYING TO ATTRACT YOUR ATTENTION.

I WANT TO LIE BACK. SHOW ME HOW THIS SEAT TIPS BACK.
CERTAINLY, SIR. JUST PRESS THIS BUTTON AND—

OOF!
OOH—I'VE GOT SOUP ALL OVER MY UNIFORM!

But—
THANKS TO THE MATERIAL I'VE USED, JUST A WIPE IS ENOUGH TO CLEAN UP ANY STAIN!
THAT'S MARVELLOUS!
Later—a mysterious hand shook some powder into the girls' jackets.
WE'LL SOON BE LANDING IN MADRID. THEN WE'LL BE ABLE TO SHOW HOW COOL THE UNIFORM STAYS IN THE HEAT.
THIS WILL MAKE THINGS HOT FOR YOU, THOUGH!
When the plane landed in Madrid—
IT DOESN'T LOOK AS IF THE UNIFORM WOULD BE SUITABLE AFTER ALL FOR WARM CLIMATES.
I DON'T UNDERSTAND THIS—I FEEL PRICKLY WHEN I SHOULD FEEL COOL.
Jane examined her jacket.
ITCHING POWDER! SOMETHING STRANGE IS GOING ON...
When the plane was ready to take off again . . .
LET ME HELP YOU WITH YOUR SAFETY BELT, SIR.

Then suddenly—
TUT TUT! THESE UNIFORMS DON'T SEEM TO BE VERY WELL MADE AT ALL.

LOOK, JANE, THE STITCHES HAVE BEEN CUT! NO WONDER IT RIPPED! SOMEONE'S TRYING TO MAKE YOU LOSE THIS AIRWAYS ORDER!

The next stop was Jamaica.
I THOUGHT THE SUN WAS SUPPOSED TO SHINE ALL THE TIME IN JAMAICA!
STILL, IT SHOWS OFF THE WATERPROOF QUALITIES OF THE UNIFORM.
BUT NONE OF THE PASSENGERS ARE INTERESTED IN IT NOW ANYWAY. THEY THINK IT'S NO GOOD. LET'S GO AND HAVE A COKE TO CHEER OURSELVES UP.
THERE'S MR CARTIER WITH ONE OF THE STEWARDESSES. HER FACE IS FAMILIAR WITH THESE DARK GLASSES ON—IF HER HAIR WAS DARK, SHE'D BE...
LET'S GET OUT OF HERE WE DON'T WANT TO BE SEEN TOGETHER.
THERE'S SOMETHING FUNNY GOING ON HERE—AND I'M GOING TO FIND OUT WHAT! COME ON, GIRLS, FOLLOW ME!
THEY'VE MADE A BREAK FOR IT. QUICK, BACK TO THE TAXI AND WE'LL FOLLOW THEM.
JANE, WHAT ARE YOU TALKING ABOUT? I DON'T UNDERSTAND.
The chase led out of town into the country, along a twisty, narrow road.
Suddenly, the leading car rounded a corner and ran into a rockslide!
AGH!

THERE'S ONLY ONE THING FOR IT—RIP UP YOUR JACKETS AND WE'LL MAKE A ROPE!
HELP! HELP! I CAN'T HOLD ON MUCH LONGER!
RIGHT, MR CARTIER, START TALKING—YOU'VE BEEN BEHIND ALL THESE "ACCIDENTS" HAVEN'T YOU?
YES, YES, I ADMIT EVERYTHING—ABOUT THE SOUP, THE ITCHING POWDER. BUT PLEASE HELP ME, PLEASE! HURRY!
MY SISTER AND I THOUGHT THAT IF WE COULD SABOTAGE YOUR UNIFORMS, THEN MY OWN COMPANY WOULD WIN THE ORDER.
YOUR SCHEME HAS SUCCEEDED, MR CARTIER. NO-ONE FROM AIRWAYS TRAVEL IS IMPRESSED BY MY UNIFORM, THANKS TO YOU.

But Jane was wrong—
WE FOLLOWED YOU WHEN WE SAW THE CAR CHASE, JANE, AND WE HEARD CARTIER ADMIT TO THE TRICKS HE PLAYED.
THE DIRECTORS HAVE DECIDED TO AWARD YOU THE CONTRACT! —YOUR NEW UNIFORMS HAVE PROVED THEIR WORTH—EVEN CARTIER WOULD AGREE WITH THAT!

HOW SUPER, JANE! AND LOOK—EVEN THE SUN IS SHINING AGAIN!
NOW WE CAN REALLY ENJOY OUR ROUND-THE-WORLD TRIP!

THE MAN IN BLACK TELLS THE STORY OF—

THE GHOST IN THE BIG TOP

The clowns received tremendous applause at the end of their act.

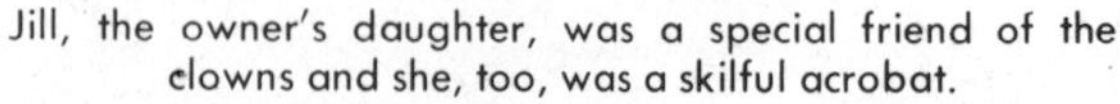
Jill, the owner's daughter, was a special friend of the clowns and she, too, was a skilful acrobat.

Just then, Mr Watson arrived.
JILL, HOW OFTEN HAVE I TOLD YOU NOT TO MIX WITH THESE CLOWNS? GO TO YOUR CARAVAN IMMEDIATELY!

STAY AWAY FROM MY DAUGHTER OR I'LL THROW YOU OUT OF THE CIRCUS. I CAN DO WITHOUT YOU, YOU KNOW!

That evening, Rico felt ill.
IF YOU'RE NOT WELL, I'LL ASK MR WATSON TO CANCEL OUR ACT TONIGHT. YOU CAN'T PERFORM WHEN YOU'RE ILL.
MR WATSON KNOWS WE CAN'T LEAVE THE CIRCUS. OTHER CIRCUSES ARE FOLDING UP EVERY DAY.
DON'T WORRY, OLD FRIEND, I'LL BE ALL RIGHT.

But when Chico asked Mr Watson . . .
CANCEL YOUR ACT? CERTAINLY NOT! RICO WAS ALL RIGHT THIS MORNING SO HE CAN PERFORM OR GET OUT!
The clowns cartwheeled into the ring to the cheers of the crowd.

Chico and Rico climbed on to the trapezes.
I HOPE RICO'S ALL RIGHT. THIS IS A DIFFICULT PART OF OUR ACT.

The clowns gave a wonderful performance.

But halfway through the routine—
AAAAGH!
WATSONS CIRCUS

RICO! RICO, SPEAK TO ME!

HE'S DEAD! YOU KILLED HIM BY FORCING HIM TO WORK WHEN HE WAS ILL!
NONSENSE! YOU COULD NEVER PROVE THAT. YOU'LL JUST HAVE TO WORK TWICE AS HARD FROM NOW ON.

Next day—

IT'S NO USE, JILL. I CAN'T GO ON.
WATSONS CIRCUS
OF COURSE YOU CAN, CHICO. YOU MUST. COME AND TEACH ME SOME NEW EXERCISES.

I WISH DADDY WASN'T SO HORRID. HE DIDN'T USE TO BE LIKE THAT. I'M SURE HE DOESN'T REALLY MEAN TO BE SO GREEDY AND NASTY.
HMM, PERHAPS IF HE WERE TAUGHT A LESSON.

JILL REALLY IS A VERY GOOD ACROBAT. THAT GIVES ME AN IDEA...

LISTEN CAREFULLY, JILL, I HAVE A PLAN...

Later—
THERE! RICO'S COSTUME FITS YOU PERFECTLY. NOW, ARE YOU SURE YOU WANT TO GO THROUGH WITH THIS?
YES, CHICO, IT WILL BE WORTH IT IF DADDY BECOMES HIS OLD SELF AGAIN.

AND LOOK, CHICO, TO MAKE IT EFFECTIVE, I'VE GOT A TIN OF LUMINOUS POWDER. IT WILL GIVE THE COSTUME A GHOSTLY APPEARANCE.

IF YOU HIDE UP IN THAT PART OF THE ROOF, YOU CAN LEAP ON TO THE TRAPEZE WHEN I'M DOING MY ACT.
AND IT WILL LOOK AS IF THE GHOST OF RICO HAS COME BACK TO HAUNT THE CIRCUS!

So, that evening as Chico was about to enter the ring—
I HOPE JILL'S IN HER PLACE BY NOW.

Chico began his act, skipping along the highwire towards the darkest part of the roof of the big top . . .
ANY SECOND NOW...
Right on time, the 'ghostly' figure swung into the act. Mr Watson was really scared.
IT—IT CAN'T BE! IT'S RICO, COME BACK FROM THE DEAD!
JILL'S PERFORMING VERY WELL, JUST AS IF SHE'D BEEN DOING IT FOR YEARS.
When Chico finished his act, his 'ghostly' companion disappeared once more into the darkness of the big top.
WE REALLY PUT ON A SHOW FOR JILL'S FATHER—AND JILL WAS AS GOOD AS RICO HIMSELF!
SUPERB!
FANTASTIC!
MORE, MORE!
Then, as Chico left the ring, he met Jill!
OH, CHICO, I'M SO SORRY I COULDN'T COME, DADDY SENT ME INTO TOWN FOR A MESSAGE AND I'VE JUST GOT BACK.
JUST GOT BACK? BUT—BUT WHO WAS THE CLOWN THAT WORKED THE ACT WITH ME JUST NOW?
WATSONS CIRCUS
WHAT DO YOU THINK, GIRLS? WAS IT JUST CHICO AND MR WATSON'S IMAGINATION—OR DID RICO GIVE A FAREWELL PERFORMANCE? WHATEVER IT WAS, MR WATSON BECAME A MUCH NICER PERSON—AND LET JILL TEAM UP WITH CHICO TO MAKE A GREAT ACT.

CALIFORNIA-
HERE WE COME!
THE Abominable Snowmen, the pop group 'adopted' by the Honourable Annalisa Murray-Clarke, are now the most popular group in the country . . .

Annalisa's father, the Earl of Balnahaven, also took an interest in the group.
ANNALISA! THAT WAS SAMUEL WEST ON THE TELEPHONE JUST NOW. HE WANTS THE "SNOWMEN" TO APPEAR ON THE TED MULLIGAN SHOW IN AMERICA IN TWO WEEKS' TIME!
GOSH, DADDY, THAT'S THE BIGGEST "LIVE" TELEVISION SHOW IN CALIFORNIA! IT COMES STRAIGHT FROM HOLLYWOOD!

At the boys' flat.
YOU'RE HAVING US ON, ANNALISA! THE TED MULLIGAN SHOW!
HONESTLY, MICK, I'M NOT! IT'S THE TRUTH!
WOWEE!

One evening, when Annalisa arrived home . . .

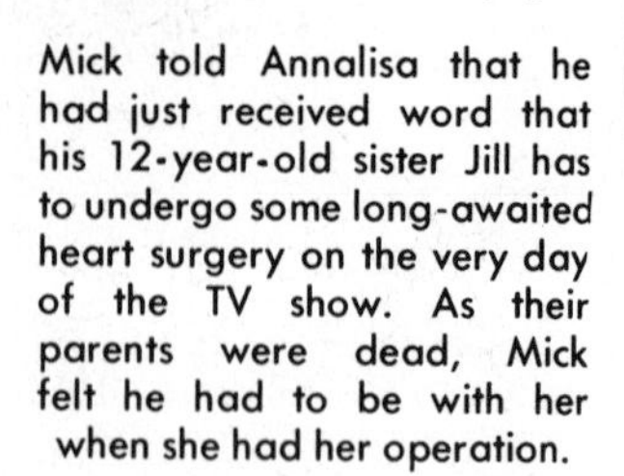

Mick told Annalisa that he had just received word that his 12-year-old sister Jill has to undergo some long-awaited heart surgery on the very day of the TV show. As their parents were dead, Mick felt he had to be with her when she had her operation.

Annalisa had to break the news to the other Snowmen.
I THOUGHT MICK WAS VERY QUIET THIS MORNING. CAN'T YOU MAKE HIM CHANGE HIS MIND, ANNALISA? WE WON'T GET ANOTHER CHANCE LIKE THIS, EVER AGAIN.
Later, Mick arrived back at the flat.
I'VE JUST BEEN ROUND AT THE HOSPITAL. THEY THINK JILL WILL BE ALL RIGHT AFTER THE OPERATION. OH, LOOK, GUYS, I'M SORRY—
FORGET IT, MICK. NATURALLY WE'RE ALL DISAPPOINTED, BUT WE KNOW HOW MUCH YOUR SISTER MEANS TO YOU.
Annalisa told her father what had happened.
MAYBE IF I EXPLAINED TO MR WEST WHAT HAD HAPPENED—
YOU COULD DO THAT, ANNALISA, BUT I DOUBT IF IT WOULD DO ANY GOOD. THESE ARE BUSY, IMPORTANT PEOPLE WE'RE DEALING WITH. THEY WON'T PUT THEMSELVES TO ANY TROUBLE OVER THE LIKES OF US.
ALL THE SAME, DADDY, THERE'S JUST A CHANCE...
Next day, at Samuel West's office . . .
THERE'S A MISS MURRAY-CLARKE TO SEE YOU, SIR. SHE SAYS IT'S IMPORTANT.
WHO? NEVER HEARD OF HER! OH WELL, SHOW HER IN. MIGHT AS WELL SEE WHAT SHE HAS TO SAY FOR HERSELF.
NOW, WHAT'S ALL THIS ABOUT?
THANK YOU FOR SEEING ME, MR WEST. I'M THE MANAGER OF THE ABOMINABLE SNOWMEN. AS YOU REMEMBER, YOU BOOKED THEM TO APPEAR ON THE TED MULLIGAN SHOW IN CALIFORNIA!
SO I DID. BUT IT WASN'T YOU I MADE THE DEAL WITH. IT WAS SOME DUKE OR SOMETHING—
THE EARL OF BALNAHAVEN. HE'S MY FATHER. THE THING IS, MR WEST, THE GROUP NOW FIND THEY ARE UNABLE TO APPEAR ON THE AGREED DATE, AND—I THAT IS, WE, WONDERED IF YOU COULD FIT THEM IN AT A LATER DATE—
LOOK, LITTLE LADY, WE'RE PUTTING ON A VERY POWERFUL TELEVISION SHOW, NOT A KINDERGARTEN CHRISTMAS SHOW. WE TELL PEOPLE WHEN TO APPEAR—THEY DON'T COME AND TELL US WHEN IT'S SUITABLE FOR THEM TO APPEAR—
ALL RIGHT, MR WEST. YOU'VE MADE YOURSELF VERY CLEAR. I SUPPOSE I SHOULD HAVE REALISED A CHILD'S LIFE ISN'T AS IMPORTANT AS YOUR PRECIOUS T V. SHOW—
NOW, HOLD ON A MINUTE! WHAT'S ALL THIS ABOUT A CHILD'S LIFE?

Annalisa told Mr West all about Mick and his sister, Jill.
AND THAT'S THE REASON THE GROUP CAN'T PLAY. NOW IF YOU DON'T MIND I SHALL GO!
NOW, JUST YOU HOLD ON A MINUTE. THIS PUTS A DIFFERENT LIGHT ON THINGS. GO AND WAIT IN THE OUTER OFFICE. I MAY BE ABLE TO HELP YOU.
NEWS
D. J. WEST
DIRECTOR
WHAT ON EARTH IS HE DOING? THE SUSPENSE IS KILLING ME!
After what seemed an age, Mr West had good news for Annalisa.
I'VE JUST BEEN ON THE PHONE TO MR MULLIGAN IN HOLLYWOOD. HE IS EVEN MORE KEEN FOR THE GROUP TO APPEAR ON HIS SHOW, AND THIS IS HOW HE PROPOSES TO DO IT—
MICK IS TO PRE-RECORD THE SONGS HE WOULD HAVE SUNG ON THE SHOW. THE OTHER THREE WILL FLY OUT AS ARRANGED, AND GO ON STAGE. AS THEY PLAY, MICK'S FILM OF HIM SINGING WILL BE SHOWN IN THE BACKGROUND.
BUT THAT'S GREAT, MR WEST! JUST GREAT!
A couple of nights later, the Snowmen held a party.
EVERYTHING IS FIXED FOR THE TRIP—AND MICK HAS TO BE AT THE STUDIO TOMORROW.
GOOD OLD ANNALISA. DON'T KNOW WHAT THE SNOWMEN WOULD DO WITHOUT HER.
Next day, Mick went down to the studios to pre-record his spot for the TV show.
STUDIO
MICK, YOU WERE MARVELLOUS!
I'M GLAD IT'S OVER, ANNALISA. WOULD YOU DROP ME OFF AT THE HOSPITAL ON THE WAY HOME, PLEASE?

Next day Annalisa and her father went down to the airport to see the Snowmen off to America . . .
CALIFORNIA—HERE WE COME!
BOAC
BOAC
JET 4
LONDON
A few days later, Annalisa was at Jill's bedside. The operation had been a success . . .
I'M SO GLAD YOU WERE ABLE TO STAY NEAR, ME, MICK.
DON'T GO TO SLEEP JUST YET, JILL. WE'VE GOT A SPECIAL SURPRISE FOR YOU!
BY NOW, YOU WILL HAVE ALL READ THE HEART-WARMING STORY BEHIND MY NEXT GUESTS' APPEARANCE. BEFORE I INTRODUCE THEM, MAY I SAY TO MISS JILLY THOMAS THAT I WISH HER A SPEEDY RECOVERY—
OH, MICK! YOU'RE JUST THE MOST WONDERFUL PERSON IN THE WHOLE WIDE WORLD! ANNALISA TOLD ME THE WHOLE STORY. I'M GOING TO GET WELL AGAIN—JUST FOR YOU!
COURSE YOU'LL GET WELL AGAIN, LOVE, AND I THINK WE SHOULD BOTH THANK ANNALISA. IT'S BECAUSE OF HER EVERYTHING'S WORKED OUT SO WELL.
THE END

Dishes for all Seasons

That's what you'll find in this special 2-page cookery section. The recipes are fun, easy to do, and are quite delicious—whatever the time of year!

SPRING

LANCASHIRE HOT POT

1 lb. middle or best end of neck of lamb, cut into cutlets.
4 medium, sliced onions.
1 tablespoon seasoned flour.
1½ lb. potatoes, sliced.
2 lamb kidneys, skinned, cored and sliced.
¾ pint stock (made with beef cube).
chopped parsley.

Trim the lamb of any excess fat, and coat with seasoned flour. Place layers of meat, onion, kidneys, mushrooms and potatoes in a large (5 pint) casserole, finishing with a layer of potatoes. Add the stock, cover, and bake in a moderate oven 350F.—Gas 4, for 2 hours. Remove the lid and cook for a further ½ hour to brown the potatoes. Serve sprinkled with chopped parsley.

EASTER DAY BOUQUETS

8 oz. plain flour.
4 oz. butter or margarine.
pinch salt.
3 oz. caster sugar.
½ level teaspoon baking powder.
2 oz. prepared almond paste.
beaten egg to bind.
caster sugar to dredge.
2 oz. glace cherries.

Sift flour, salt and baking powder in a bowl. Rub in butter or margarine, stir in sugar, then bind to a fairly firm dough with beaten egg. Equally divide mixture into 16 small balls, and pat into rounds. Wash, dry, and cut the cherries in halves. Place a cherry on each piece of almond paste, then set on to dough rounds, forming each one into a small ball to completely enclose the almond paste and cherry. Place on greased baking sheet. Press down with back of fork, bake in a hot oven 425 deg. F.—Mark 7 for 15 minutes, or till cooked through.

SUMMER

Summer and salads go together like Punch and Jud or Laurel and Hardy. Here are some rather different on for you to try, and while you're at it, why not have a go making your own mayonnaise?

MAYONNAISE

2 egg yolks.
1 teaspoon caster sugar.
½ level teaspoon each salt, pepper and dry mustard.
3 dessertspoons wine vineg
½ pint olive oil.

Place the egg yolks in a bowl. Add sugar, salt, pepper mustard. Then graduall add the vinegar—measuring out drop by drop. Next add the oil, whiski mixture all the time. It should now be a smooth consistency. If the mayonnaise is n to be used for a time, add 2 tablespoons boiling water. Store in a cool place.

RAINBOW SALAD

4 red skinned apples.
1-2 lemons.
3 sticks celery.
2 oz. chopped walnu
2 tablespoons single cream, or top of the milk.
Few crisp lettuce leaves.
Seasoning to taste.

Wash, dry and core apples, cut into slices or cubes (leave peel on to preve discolouration.) Put into bowl, and sprinkle with lemon juice. Wash and cut cele Add celery, along with chopped walnuts, to apples. Mix mayonnaise with single cre or top of milk, and pour over the ingredients in the bowl. Toss lightly, and a seasoning. Next, line a salad bowl with the lettuce leaves. Pour in the salad mixtu and garnish with remaining apple and chopped walnuts. To use this salad as a m course, serve along with cold meat or cheese.

FLORIDA SALAD

Line a round dish with lettuce leaves. Place on this halved pineapple slic orange sections, tinned grapefruit segments, and sliced bananas. Add abou tablespoon of whipped cream to some of your prepared mayonnaise, and pour o salad.

STUFFED TOMATO SALAD

6 medium sized tomatoes.
Spring onions.
Mayonnaise.
diced, cooked carrot.
Chopped parsley.
cooked peas.
diced, cooked potato.
Lettuce.

Cut the top off each tomato, and scoop out the pulp. Mix together the vegetab and finely chopped onions. Add sufficient salad cream to make the mixture bind w Fill the tomato cases with this salad, and sprinkle a little parsley over the to each. Place on a dish lined with small pieces of lettuce.

sweet Summer days, some sweet Summer sserts . . .

BANANA CARNIVAL

fully ripe bananas.
oz. caster sugar.
ice of ½ a lemon.
pint cream or evaporated milk.
oz. toasted chopped almonds.
ace cherries.

Mash the bananas with sugar and lemon juice. nip up the cream or evaporated milk until it is ick, and fold in the banana mixture. Spoon into ndae glasses, sprinkle with almonds, and place a cherry on top of each.

BAKED ALASKA

sponge cake.
family-sized block vanilla ice-cream.
oz. caster sugar.
egg whites.
pinch of cream of tartar.

Scoop out the centre of the sponge cake, aving the base about ½-1 inch thick, and pile me stiffly frozen ice-cream into the centre. Add e cream of tartar to the egg-whites, whisk until iff, and fold in the sugar. Line a baking tray with ease-proof paper, and place the cake on this. oat the outside of the cake and the ice cream with e meringue mixture, making sure the cake is mpletely covered. Pop into a hot oven 450 deg.F. -mark 8 and leave for 3-4 minutes, until the meringue is lightly coloured.

AUTUMN

Autumn is the time for apples, kite-flying, chestnut gathering and suppers round the fire. Here is a simple menu which you can easily make—giving Mum a well-earned rest.

TOMATO RAREBIT

¼ pint milk ½ oz. flour Cayenne pepper
¼ pint thick tomato puree 3 oz. grated cheese
Buttered toast 1 oz. butter 1 egg

Melt the butter and stir in the flour smoothly. Gradually add the milk and tomato puree (this you can make yourself by rubbing fresh or tinned tomatoes through a sieve.) Add the grated cheese, season with pepper. Stir in the beaten egg without allowing mixture to boil, pour over pieces of buttered toast, and serve very hot.

APPLE SNAPS

4 large slices white bread 3-4 oz. butter
1 heaped tablespoon demerara sugar
1 medium-sized cooking apple
¼ level teaspoon cinnamon powder

Melt the butter in a small pan. Remove the crusts from the bread, and cut each slice in half. Brush the bread on both sides with the melted butter. Next, peel, core and thinly slice the cooking apple, place in a basin, and mix with the sugar and cinnamon.

Place four of the half slices of bread on a baking sheet, and cover with the prepared apple. Place the remaining slices of bread firmly on top. Put in a hot oven (375 deg.F. Gas Mark 5) on the top shelf, and cook for twenty minutes until lightly browned.

Serve hot with whipped cream, custard sauce or ice cream.

WINTER

Whatever kind of fowl you had for Christmas Day dinner, it gets very boring eating it roasted with vegetables all the time. Here are a few ideas to spice up the bird a bit, and make every meal seem special. We have used turkey in our recipes, but you can substitute that with whatever you like, chicken, duck, goose etc.

TURKEY OMELETTE

Ideally, omelettes should be cooked individually, and eaten at once. For a one person omelette, you need:-
2 eggs, diced turkey, 1 tablespoon milk and seasoning, ½ oz. butter.

Heat the ½ oz. butter in a pan until hot. Pour in the beaten eggs, stirring the mixture once or twice with a fork, until just set. It is at this point you add your turkey spreading it over the middle of the omelette. Use a palette knife, and carefully fold the omelette in half. Leave to cook for a few moments, and then very carefully turn the omelette over on the other side, again leaving to cook for a few moments. Serve immediately.

TURKEY FLAN

2 rashers streaky bacon (chopped). 1 small onion (chopped).
1½ oz. butter or margarine. 8 oz. cooked, diced turkey.
1 Chicken Stock Cube dissolved in ½ pint boiling water. 1½ oz. plain flour.
1 level teaspoon parsley. 1 small can evaporated milk.
1-8 inch cooked flan case (made with 6 oz. shortcrust pastry).
To decorate—2 large sliced tomatoes.

Fry the bacon in a pan until lightly browned. Remove from heat. Next, fry the onion until cooked, but not brown. In a saucepan, melt the butter, then add the flour and leave to cook for a minute. Take from heat, and gradually stir in the stock cube and evaporated milk. Return to heat, bring to boil, stirring continuously. Leave to cook for a minute, add seasoning, chicken, bacon onions and parsley. Pour into flan case, and decorate with tomato.

CHRISTMAS MEDLEY

Cabbage; Turkey; Carrots; Apples; Sultanas; Grated Cheese; Chopped Walnuts.

Carefully wash and shred the carrots and cabbage. Peel, core and slice apples. Wash sultanas, and cut turkey into strips. In a large salad bowl, make the first layer of carrots and cabbage; next add the sultanas, apples and walnuts. Top with turkey and cheese. Repeat layers until all the ingredients have been used.

HI, THERE! I'M BELLE OF THE BALL!

Then—

WHERE'S MY LITTLE PET TODAY, THEN? AW! IS SHE SHY?

GULP!

SWOON

Later, when Auntie had gone.
THAT WAS VERY NAUGHTY—THOUGH, I MUST ADMIT, AUNT PRUNELLA GIVES ME A PAIN!

From that moment on, she was called "Belle of the Ball!"

And now, back to the present . . .
I ALWAYS SAY—CAN'T GET INTO MUCH TROUBLE WITH A BALL!

OOPS! DAD'S PRIZE MARROWS! I SPOKE TOO SOON!
SQUELCH!

IT'S the year 1746. Prince Charles Edward Stuart has lost his last battle for his father's throne at Culloden.

Prince Charles has escaped and is thought to be hiding somewhere in the Hebrides.

In one small cottage on one of the many Hebridean islands, a girl wakes up in the night.

She is fourteen-year-old Sarah MacLeod . . .

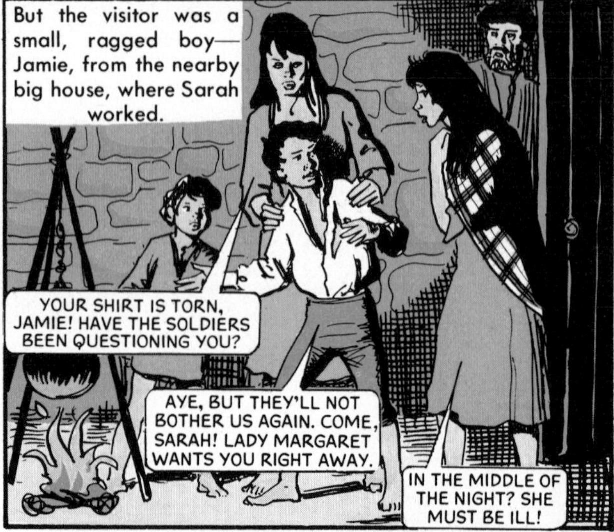

The Redcoats insisted on searching Lady Margaret's house.
I MUST PRETEND TO AID LADY MARGARET. HER FIRST GLANCE WARNED ME THAT SHE WASN'T ILL BUT THAT I MUST REMAIN SILENT.

When the soldiers at last left, Lady Margaret took Sarah to the small sewing room.
I HAVE A MOST IMPORTANT TASK FOR YOU, SARAH.
I AM TO SEW THEN— IN THE MIDDLE OF THE NIGHT!

I WANT YOU TO SEW ME A LADY'S OUTFIT FROM THIS MATERIAL.
BUT THIS IS NOT FIT FOR A LADY'S DRESS, MA'AM— IT'S TOO DULL...

Lady Margaret insisted it was just what she wanted.
YOU SEW THE FINEST STITCH IN ALL THE HEBRIDES, SARAH. I MUST BEG YOU TO KEEP WORKING TILL THE GARMENTS ARE READY.
I SHALL DO MY BEST, LADY MARGARET.

THIS LADY MUST BE VERY TALL. I'M SURE THIS DRESS IS ALL OF TWO YARDS LONG.
For two days and nights, with only brief rests, Sarah sewed. There was one interruption . . .
I TOLD YOU, THIS CHILD IS NO SPY. CHARLES STUART CHOOSES HIS HELPERS CAREFULLY.
I'D FIGHT FOR THE PRINCE GIVEN THE CHANCE!

At last the clothes were ready.
YOU HAVE DONE WELL, SARAH. NOW TAKE THEM TO MISS FLORA MACDONALD. THEY'RE FOR HER MAID, BETTY BURKE.
Miss MacDonald also thanked Sarah warmly.
I WONDER WHY MISS MACDONALD'S TALL MAID DIDN'T ANSWER THE DOOR? I LONGED TO SEE HER.
Sarah returned home and told her parents her story.
...AND THAT WAS ALL, MOTHER. WHERE'S ALEXANDER?
Sarah's brother, Alexander, was tending the sheep.
HE FORGOT HIS FOOD, SARAH. WILL YOU TAKE IT TO HIM? THE FRESH AIR WILL DO YOU GOOD.
Alexander was nowhere in sight. Sarah sat down for a rest.
I'M SURE THAT'S MY COUSIN NEIL DOWN THERE. HE CAN'T BE GOING FISHING AT THIS HOUR. I'LL GO AND TALK TO HIM TILL ALEXANDER COMES.
By the time Sarah reached the beach, another person had arrived—Miss Flora MacDonald.
THAT'S A FINE BOAT, NEIL. WHERE ARE YOU TAKING HER AT THIS HOUR? OH, MISS MACDONALD...
SARAH! GO! GO QUICKLY!
NO. LET HER STAY. I WANT HER TO MEET MY MAID, BETTY BURKE.

At that moment "Betty Burke" appeared.
WHAT ARE YOU DOING?
I'M HONOURED TO MEET THE CREATOR OF MY EXCELLENT DISGUISE. YOU HAVE MY GRATEFUL THANKS.
IT'S THE PRINCE!
Soon—
AND THE SOLDIERS THOUGHT I WAS TOO STUPID TO HELP THE PRINCE. IF THEY BUT KNEW...BUT THEY NEVER SHALL FROM ME!
Sarah told no-one her secret—not even her mother.
SPREAD THE NEWS! THE PRINCE HAS ESCAPED SAFELY!
HE MUST HAVE BEEN WELL DISGUISED TO ESCAPE FROM THIS ISLAND!
And, some time later—
I HAVE NEWS TODAY THAT THE PRINCE HAS LANDED SAFELY IN FRANCE. HE IS SAFE FOREVER. NO SMALL THANKS TO...A GIRL CALLED SARAH!

ESCAPE

TO THE NEW FOREST

The year is 1647, and King Charles I has been defeated in the Civil War against the Parliamentary Army under Oliver Cromwell. The King was imprisoned at Hampton Court, but has escaped and is believed to be hiding in the region of the New Forest. To the south of the New Forest is a large property called Arnwood, the home of the Beverley family. Colonel Beverley was killed at the Battle of Naseby, and his four children, Edward, Humphrey, Alice and Edith live at Arnwood under the guardianship of their elderly Aunt Judith.

Fire and Smoke

THE cottage of Jacob Armitage was situated about a mile from Arnwood. When Colonel Beverley had joined the King's troops, he had begged the old man to watch for the safety of his wife and children. The death of Colonel Beverley was a heavy blow to the old forester, but, when Mrs Beverley followed her husband to the grave, he redoubled his attention, and was seldom more than a few hours away from the mansion.

As soon as the escape of the King was made known, Cromwell's troops descended on the New Forest. They were subdivided, and ordered to scour every inch of the forest in groups of twelve to twenty men.

One day, as old Jacob was out hunting for some venison, a party of Cromwell's Roundheads rode past. The old man hid behind some bushes; after all, he was a King's forester, and even that in those troubled times could mean danger.

"We are approaching Arnwood," he heard one of the soldiers observe.

"Arnwood?" replied another, "Is that not the property of Cavalier Beverley who was shot down at Naseby?"

"The King might well be concealed in that house," observed another.

"Searching their houses is useless!" cried the leader. "What with their spring panels and secret doors, their false ceilings and double walls, one may ferret forever and find nothing."

"Yes," replied another, "their abodes are full of these abominations; but there is one way which is sure; and if the man Charles is concealed in any house, I venture to say that I will find him. Fire and smoke will bring him forth; and to every Cavalier's house within twenty miles I will apply the torch. We must set Arnwood alight at night!"

The troopers sprang upon their saddles and went off at a hard trot. Jacob remained among the fern until they were out of sight, and then rose up. He went first to his cottage to deposit his gun, saddled his forest pony, and set off for Arnwood.

"I shall have a difficult job with the stiff old lady," thought Jacob as he rang the bell; "I don't believe she would rise out of her high chair for old Noll and his whole army at his back. But we shall see."

The Lady of the House

IN a few minutes, Jacob was ushered up into Miss Judith Villiers' apartment. The old lady was about fifty years of age, very prim and starched, sitting in her high-backed chair, with her feet upon a stool and her hands crossed before her.

"You have important business with us, I am told," observed Miss Judith.

"Most important," madam," replied Jacob. "In the first place, it is right that you should be informed that His Majesty King Charles has escaped from Hampton Court."

"His Majesty escaped!" replied the lady.

"Yes, and is supposed to be secreted in this neighbourhood. His Majesty is not in this house, madam, I presume?"

"Jacob, his Majesty is not in this house; if he were, I would suffer my tongue to be cut out sooner than I would confess it, even to you."

Jacob then entered into the details of what he had overheard that morning, concluding with the information that the mansion would be burned down that night. He then pointed out the necessity of immediately abandoning the house, as it would be impossible to oppose the troopers.

"Jacob, I shall remain here," replied the old lady with dignified calm. "I shall remain in this very chair."

"But, madam, the children cannot remain here. I will not leave them here. I promised the Colonel . . ."

"Will the children be in more danger than I shall be, Jacob Armitage?" replied the old lady stiffly. "They dare not ill-treat me

adapted from "CHILDREN OF THE NEW FOREST" by CAPTAIN MARRYAT.

— they may force the buttery and drink the ale; but they will hardly dare to insult a lady of the house of Villiers."

"I fear they will dare anything, madam. At all events, they will frighten the children, and, for one night, they will be better in my cottage."

Jacob's Ruse

JACOB then went in search of them, and found them playing in the garden. He called to the two boys, and told them to follow him.

"Now, Mr Edward," said he, "you must prove yourself your father's own son. We must leave this house immediately; come up with me to your rooms, and help me to pack up yours and your sisters' clothes, for we must go to my cottage this night. There is no time to be lost."

"But why, Jacob? I must know why."

"Because the Parliamentary troopers will burn it down this night."

"Burn it down! Why, the house is mine, is it not? Who dares to burn down this house?"

"They will dare and will do it."

"But we will fight them, Jacob; we can bolt and bar; I can fire a gun and hit, too, as you know."

"It is impossible, my dear boy. Remember your sisters. Would you have them burned to death, or shot by these wretches?"

But Edward Beverley required more persuasion to abandon the house. At last old Jacob prevailed, and the clothes were tied up in bundles.

"Now we will carry down the bundles, and you make them fast on the pony while I go for your sisters," said Jacob.

"But where does Aunt Judith go?" enquired Edward.

"She will not leave the house, Master Edward; she intends to stay and speak to the troopers."

"And so an old woman like her remains to face the enemy, while I run away from them!" replied Edward. "I will not go."

"Well, Master Edward," replied Jacob, "you must do as you please; but it will be cruel to leave your sisters here; they and Humphrey must come with me, and I cannot manage to get them to the cottage without your help."

To this Edward consented. The pony was soon loaded, and the little girls, who were still playing in the garden, were called in. They were told that they were going to pass the night in the cottage, and were delighted at the idea.

"Now, Master Edward," said Jacob, "will you take your sisters by the hand and lead them to the cottage? Here is the key of the door; Master Humphrey can lead the pony; and, Master Edward," continued Jacob, taking him aside, "I'll tell you one thing which I will not mention before your brothers and sisters: the troopers are all about the New Forest, looking for the King. You must not leave your brother and sisters till I return. Lock the cottage door as soon as it is dark. I will remain here to see what I can do with your aunt."

Arnwood Burns

THIS latter ruse of Jacob's succeeded. Edward promised that he would not leave his sisters, and it was nearly dark when the little party quitted the mansion of Arnwood. All the servants had flown, but Miss Judith refused to listen to Jacob's entreaties to come with him.

"Leave me, Jacob Armitage, and shut the door when you go out," were her parting words.

Jacob hung around in the region of the house until the troopers arrived. They surrounded the mansion, and shortly afterwards he perceived the glare of torches and, in quarter of an hour, thick smoke rose up in the dark but clear sky. At last the flames burst forth from the lower windows of the mansion, and soon afterwards they lighted up the country round to some distance.

"It is done," thought Jacob, and he turned towards his own cottage. Suddenly, he heard the galloping of a horse and violent screams. A minute afterwards, a soldier passed him with the old lady tied behind him, kicking and struggling as hard as she could. So Miss Judith was safe! It was evident that the soldier who had her imagined that she was King Charles dressed up as an old woman.

In half an hour, Jacob had passed through the thick woods which separated his cottage from Arnwood. He knocked at the door and Edward answered.

"My sisters are in bed and fast asleep," he said, "and Humphrey has been nodding this past half hour. I'll go back to Arnwood now that you have returned."

"Come out, Master Edward," replied Jacob, "and look." Edward saw the flames and fierce light between the trees and was silent.

"I told you that it would be so, and you would all have been burnt in your beds, for they did not enter the house to see who was in it, but fired it as soon as they had surrounded it."

"And my aunt?" exclaimed Edward, clasping his hands.

"Is safe, Master Edward, and by this time at Lymington."

Edward slowly followed Jacob into the cottage. They had escaped, but his little heart was full. He had lost both his parents, and now his home, but when he grew to be a man, he would rebuild it. He was sure of that.

TRAINING A YOUNG PONY

To train a young pony you must have patience, sympathy and a lot of nerve and determination. You must also be good natured, for if you lose your temper you may lose control of your pony, too.

Obviously you must be able to ride reasonably well to put the message over to your pony but there's no harm in seeking advice from someone who knows a lot on this subject. Failing this, there are many informative books on ponies and their training which you could refer to.

★ ★ ★ ★ ★

Before beginning training you should try to understand how your pony's mind works.

Because his power of reasoning is very restricted you have to rely almost entirely on his memory for training.

1. YOU HAVE TO RELY ALMOST ENTIRELY ON HIS MEMORY FOR TRAINING.

By connecting certain facts in his memory and forming habits which become almost second nature to him, you compel his obedience.

★ ★ ★ ★ ★

A pony delights in anything that gives him pleasure like eating, being petted and going at full gallop. Once you begin to share in his feelings and anticipate his next moves you are well on the way to understanding how his mind works.

A pony has a strong instinct of fear and this can be overcome by gaining his confidence. Approach your pony quietly and work slowly and gently with him, for if you are noisy you will frighten him.

He must be taught to do what you want and not what he wants, for if he gets his own way he has learnt disobedience.

2. A PONY DELIGHTS IN ANYTHING THAT GIVES HIM PLEASURE—LIKE EATING.

Never try to teach your pony something new if he's feeling tired. Wait until he is calm and collected and make sure you're not asking too much of him.

At times it won't be easy to decide whether your pony has failed to understand your meaning, if he's feeling nervous or whether he's just being naughty. Losing your temper is no way to solve this problem. Remember you must always blame yourself and not your pony.

3. YOU MUST ALWAYS BLAME YOURSELF AND NOT YOUR PONY.

If he does well, you should immediately reward your pony with some tasty titbit, but you should never punish him when you are angry. Instead, attempt to correct a fault by repeating the lesson. If punishment is really necessary it must be carried out immediately and always make certain that your pony knows what he's being punished for.

★ ★ ★ ★ ★

Another important part of a pony's training is keeping him in good condition.

4. IF YOU OVERFEED YOUR PONY HE WILL BECOME FAT AND HEAVY.

A healthy pony has an alert head with well-pricked ears and wide-open eyes. His coat should be glossy and should move easily on the ribs beneath.

If you overfeed your pony he will become fat, heavy and rather excitable. Give him adequate food to correspond with his development and avoid overstraining him with too much work.

If you ensure the right balance in conditioning, exercising and training you will gain good results with your pony.

MARY BROWN'S SCHOOLDAYS
IT'S a day like any other at St Winifred's School, and Mary Brown and her fellow third-formers are heading for the refectory for lunch.
And the girls know that lunch is going to be like any other lunch at St Win's—awful!
TODAY'S TUESDAY—THAT MEANS STEW AND DOUGHBALLS!
THE FOOD REALLY IS CHRONIC THESE DAYS!
OH, NO! I CAN'T FACE IT!
NO! NO! I CAN'T HAVE ANOTHER ST WIN'S MEAL!
I'VE JUST HAD ANOTHER GHASTLY THOUGHT. IT'S FROGSPAWN—I MEAN, TAPIOCA, TO FOLLOW! YECH!
The girls did their best to eat the food.
But—
THIS IS TERRIBLE! EVEN I CAN'T EAT THIS!
LET'S GO TO THE TUCK SHOP AND GET SOME DECENT FOOD.
They found the tuck shop closed.
TUCKSHOP
CLOSED
THE TUCK SHOP'S SOLD OUT! THE OTHER GIRLS HAVE BEATEN US TO IT!

SOMETHING MUST BE DONE ABOUT THE FOOD SITUATION, MARY! EVERY-ONE FEELS THE SAME. IT CAN'T GO ON!
I WONDER...
Next day, Mary organised a protest march.
DOWN WITH STODGY PUDDINGS
PRUNES MUST GO
NO MORE GOOEY STEW
DON'T SUFFER ST. WIN'S SAGO IN SILENCE

But the teachers walked past, unconcerned.
NO MORE GOOEY STEW
PRUNES MUST GO
HUH! THEY HAVEN'T EVEN NOTICED THAT WE'RE PROTESTING!
Mary had another plan, and, later in the third form dormitory . . .
WE'LL GET EVERYONE TO SIGN THIS PETITION ABOUT THE FOOD. THAT'LL MAKE THE STAFF SIT UP!
All that day . . .
QUICK! SIGN IT WHILE MISS MILLER'S NOT LOOKING!
At last the petition was completed.
RIGHT, MARY! IT WAS YOUR IDEA, SO IT'S UP TO YOU TO PRESENT THE PETITION TO THE HEAD!

Mary knocked at the door of the Headmistress's study.
HEADMISTRESS
WELL, HERE GOES!
She opened the door and timidly faced the Head.
YES, MARY? I'M VERY BUSY.
MM—AH—WELL—ER—
OH, STOP STUTTERING, GIRL, AND GIVE ME THAT, WHATEVER IT IS!
I'LL ATTEND TO THAT WHEN I'VE GOT TIME.
Without as much as a glance at the petition, the Headmistress tossed it on to a pile of papers.
THAT'S THE LAST WE'LL SEE OF OUR PETITION! IT'LL SOON BE BURIED THERE!

Mary reported back to the other third-formers.
SO I'M AFRAID OUR PETITION MAY NOT HAVE AN IMMEDIATE EFFECT.
WHAT? AFTER ALL OUR HARD WORK?

NEVER MIND, I'VE GOT A BETTER IDEA! WE'LL GO ON A HUNGER STRIKE! WE WON'T EAT ANOTHER THING UNTIL THEY PROMISE TO IMPROVE THE FOOD!
YES! WE'LL BEAT THEM YET!
HM! I DON'T LIKE THE SOUND OF THAT VERY MUCH!

Next day, after breakfast.
NOBODY EVEN NOTICED WE SKIPPED BREAKFAST. OUR HUNGER STRIKE ISN'T OFF TO A VERY GOOD START, AND I'M STARVING.
WE MUST BE DETERMINED, BRENDA! THEY'LL NOTICE —DON'T WORRY.
Later, in class—
HO—HUM! ANOTHER TEN MINUTES OF HISTORY TO GO. I THINK I'LL HAVE A SWEET. THE TEACHER ISN'T LOOKING.
Chocolates
CHOCOLATES
Five minutes later—
OOPS! WHAT AM I DOING? I ALMOST FORGOT ABOUT THE HUNGER SRIKE!
At the end of the history period—
WHERE'S BRENDA OFF TO?
Mary followed Brenda, and . . .
REALLY, BRENDA! LETTING US DOWN LIKE THIS! AND BEFORE ANYONE NOTICED WE WERE ON A HUNGER STRIKE TOO!
SORRY, MARY. I JUST COULDN'T KEEP IT UP ANY LONGER!
Lunchtime—
EAT UP, GIRLS! IT'S GOOD NUTRITIOUS FOOD!

Mary couldn't contain herself.
OH, MISS! IT'S AWFUL!
TAKE 100 LINES, BROWN—I MUST NOT TURN MY NOSE UP AT GOOD, WHOLESOME FOOD!
That evening, in the dormitory . . .
BETTER GET THESE LINES DONE, I SUPPOSE!
IF ONLY WE COULD HAVE ONE GOOD FEED —JUST ONE!
WHEN WAS THE LAST TIME WE HAD A GOOD FEED HERE? I CAN'T REMEMBER.
I REMEMBER. IT WAS THE TIME WE HAD THOSE CELEBRITIES VISITING THE SCHOOL. THEY PUT ON A GOOD SPREAD FOR US THEN —I SUPPOSE TO MAKE A GOOD IMPRESSION.
THAT'S IT, THEN! ALL WE NEED IS A CELEBRITY!
ALL?
YES. THAT SHOULDN'T BE TOO DIFFICULT. LET'S HAVE A LOOK AT THE PAPER.
EVENING
HERE WE ARE! MARGOT FOUNTAIN, THE BALLERINA, IS IN TOWN THIS WEEK. I'M SURE SHE'D LIKE TO SEE OUR FAMOUS SCHOOL!

BUT HOW...
OH, I'M SURE MISS LIGHT-FOOT, OUR DANCING MISTRESS WOULD INVITE HER FOR US.
So, next day, Miss Lightfoot, and Mary called on the ballerina.
OF COURSE, I'D LOVE TO VISIT ST WINIFRED'S!
OH, SUPER! THE GIRLS WILL BE DELIGHTED!
A few days later, on the day Miss Fountain was to visit the school . . .
LUNCH! COME ON!
I CAN'T WAIT!
LOOK AT THIS! FANTASTIC! JUST AS WE PLANNED!
HERE COMES MISS FOUNTAIN NOW.
NEVER MIND HER! NOSH AWAY!
HM! SHE DOESN'T LOOK TOO PLEASED!

Later, as the girls settled back after a lovely meal, the Head-mistress came in, alone.

GIRLS! MISS FOUNTAIN HAS GONE NOW—BUT BEFORE SHE WENT, SHE GAVE ME WHAT I CONSIDER TO BE VERY GOOD ADVICE...

HAVING SEEN US AT LUNCH, SHE TELLS ME THAT SHE THINKS OUR DIET HERE IS TOO STODGY AND RICH—SHE BELIEVES IN A VEGETARIAN DIET...
OH, OH!

SO, FOR A TRIAL PERIOD OF A FEW WEEKS I THINK WE AT ST WINIFRED'S SHOULD GO ON A SIMPLE VEGETABLE DIET, AND I'M SURE YOU'LL BE ONLY TOO HAPPY IF IT MAKES YOU AS FIT AND LOVELY AS MISS FOUNTAIN!

As soon as the Head had gone—
BOINK
POP
SWOOSH
IT'S ALL MARY'S FAULT!
SWISSSH
GET HER!
SPLAT
BUT...BUT, GIRLS, I GOT YOU YOUR ONE BIG FEED, DIDN'T I? HEY! STOP!

A LEAD ON DOGS

IF you are thinking of buying a dog, here are a few facts and figures about eight well-known varieties.

IRISH SETTER

COAT—Flat and soft with feathering and free from waves or curls.
COLOUR—Rich golden chestnut.
HEIGHT—24-26 inches.
WEIGHT—55-65 lb.
TAIL—Moderate length and carried level.

BEAGLE

COAT—Smooth and short.
COLOUR—Black with tan or white markings (tricolour).
HEIGHT—13-15 inches.
WEIGHT—30-40 lb.
TAIL—Thick, long and gay.

GREAT DANE

COAT—Short, thick and sleek.
COLOUR—Black, brindle and all shades of blue or fawn.
HEIGHT—Minimum of 30 inches.
WEIGHT—Minimum of 120 lb.
TAIL—Carried low.

CHOW-CHOW

COAT—Abundant with thick mane and undercoat.
COLOUR—Black, chocolate, red or blue with paler featherings.
HEIGHT—20 inches.
WEIGHT—55-60 lb.
TAIL—Well plumed and carried over the back.

DALMATIAN

COAT—Short and smooth.
COLOUR—White with liver or jet black spots.
HEIGHT—20-23 inches.
WEIGHT—45-60 lb.
TAIL—Moderate length and carried level.

WELSH CORGI (Pembrokeshire)

COAT—Medium length, smooth and dense.
COLOUR—Black-and-tan, fox-red or sable-red with or without white markings.
HEIGHT—10-11 inches.
WEIGHT—20-22 lb.
TAIL—Short or absent.

SHETLAND SHEEPDOG

COAT—Long with frills and feathering.
COLOUR—Tan-and-white, sable, sable-and-white, tricolour, black-and-tan and blue-merle.
HEIGHT—12-15 inches.
WEIGHT—14 lb.
TAIL—Soft feathered brush.

DACHSHUND

COAT—Short, smooth and close-lying.
COLOUR—Chocolate-and-tan, black-and-tan, liver, red and dapple.
HEIGHT—8-10 inches.
WEIGHT—10-25 lb.
TAIL—Long and tapering.

THE PONY WHO LIKED FUN

FREDA BARNES loves ponies and her ambition is to some-day become a first class show-jumper.

After a year of weekly riding lessons her father decides to buy her a pony of her own.

The following Saturday . . .
IT'S THE SHOWING CLASS FIRST, AND WE MUST DO OUR BEST.
With the other riders Freda on Dinky walked, trotted, cantered and galloped round the ring watched by the judges.
21
Dinky was first in line for inspection . . .
THAT'S A VERY SMART TURN OUT, MISS BARNES.
But as the judges were about to move on, Dinky began to play up.
DINKY, LEAVE THE JUDGE'S HAT ALONE—OH NO!
Freda and Dinky were sent from the ring.
OH, HOW COULD YOU, DINKY? JUST WHEN WE WERE DOING SO WELL. LOOK AT THAT CROWD LAUGHING AT US. WHAT A DISGRACE!
WE
PON
But Freda didn't give up easily and entered for the jumping test.
YOU'VE JUMPED WELL AT HOME, DINKY. IT'S OUR TURN NOW. WE'LL SHOW THEM YOU CAN DO IT.

Dinky began very well and cleared the fences with ease.
GOOD BOY, YOU'RE DOING WELL!
Then for no reason at all he dodged round a couple of fences and Freda lost control.
STOP IT, OH, PLEASE BEHAVE!
Next Dinky decided he was thirsty.
RIGHT IN THE MIDDLE OF THE WATER JUMP. OH, I'LL NEVER LIVE THIS DOWN.
Later back at the horsebox Freda lost her temper.
YOU ARE A STUPID HORSE! MAKE A FOOL OUT OF ME WOULD YOU? I'LL TEACH YOU!
But just then another young rider appeared.
HEY! THERE'S NO NEED TO TREAT YOUR PONY LIKE THAT. GIVE ME THAT WHIP! HE'S ONLY A YOUNG PONY AND HAS OBVIOUSLY HAD LITTLE SHOWING EXPERIENCE.
YOU MIND YOUR OWN BUSINESS!

LOOK, LET ME HELP YOU— AND YOUR PONY!
OH, PLEASE DO! I WANT SO MUCH TO DO WELL.

The girl introduced herself as Susan Moore.
YOU'RE A MEMBER OF THE PONY CLUB AREN'T YOU, FREDA?
YES, BUT HOW CAN THAT HELP ME?
YOU COULD COME ALONG TO THEIR PONY CLUB CAMP WITH ME NEXT WEEK. THERE YOU COULD GET SOME EXTRA TUITION WHICH WOULD IMPROVE YOUR RIDING AND DINKY'S BEHAVIOUR.
So a week later Freda joined Susan at Pony Club Camp.
THIS IS MY PONY, NIMBLE, FREDA. LET ME INTRODUCE YOU TO SOME OF THE OTHERS.
PONY CLUB

In the afternoon Freda and Dinky went along with the other riders and their ponies for some instruction.
NOW I WANT YOU TO RIDE ROUND IN A CIRCLE AND WHEN I ASK YOU TO GALLOP, DO SO UNTIL I TELL YOU STOP. RIGHT, OFF YOU GO!

But little, playful Dinky was determined not to ride round in a circle.
COME ON, DINKY. DON'T LET ME DOWN AGAIN.

Then the instructress changed the order to gallop.
THAT'S BETTER, BOY. YOU'RE WELL AHEAD OF THE OTHERS.

OUCH!
But when they were told to stop, Dinky came to such a sudden halt that Freda sailed over his head.

YOU'LL HAVE TO HANG ON BETTER THE NEXT TIME, YOUNG LADY.
NEVER MIND THE OTHERS, FREDA. UP YOU GET!
As the week went by Freda and Dinky's performance grew steadily worse.
LOOK AT THE MESS THEY'RE MAKING OF THE JUMPING COURSE.
Freda was very upset.
OH, DINKY, IT LOOKS LIKE WE'RE BOTH HOPELESS. I GIVE UP!
OH, SNAP OUT OF THE MISERIES, FREDA. I'VE PUT YOUR NAME DOWN FOR THE MOUNTED GAMES THIS AFTERNOON, SO YOU MUST HAVE A GO. IT'LL CHEER YOU BOTH UP. IT'S GREAT FUN.

Over the next few months Freda and Dinky, with the rest of the team, won through all the qualifying rounds held at various gymkhanas throughout the country.

KATE GOES SHOPPING

HOW TO PLAY

Any number of people can take part. All you need is a button or counter each and a dice.

Throw a six to start. Then follow Kate through the department store to the finish in the boutique on the fourth floor.

Have fun—Kate did!

START
Tangled in swing-doors—miss a turn.
HARDW RE
Accident in the china department—miss two turns.
Managed to catch the lift—move to square 23.
TOYS & SP RTS
Sidetracked in toy department—miss a turn.
Catch the escalator—move to 29.
COFFEE BAR
Meet some friends in the coffee bar—miss two turns.
Avoid over-suspicious store detective—move to 21.
Catch lift, but it's on the way down—return to 8.
1
2
3
4
5
6
7
8
9
10
11
12
13
14
15
16
17
18
19
20
21
22

SAMMY GOES TO SEA

JEANETTE placed her exercise and text books carefully away in the drawer of the wooden cabinet. Her mother and father were members of a travelling circus, and so she did most of her school work at home in their caravan.

Jeanette could never attend a regular school for more than a week or a fortnight, depending upon how long the circus stayed in town, but her mother, who trained the performing sea lions, and her father, who was Noggin, the Clown, both saw to it that Jeanette did full time studies and so she was as quick and bright as any other schoolgirl of her age.

Jeanette was also an accomplished trapeze and tightrope artist and appeared in almost every performance, swinging at a dizzy height from one trapeze bar to another, and working on the ropes with all the grace and ease of a ballerina.

None of this held any fear for Jeanette. But she did have one fear—water! It wasn't that Jeanette couldn't swim, for she had learned at an early age.

However, one day at the swimming baths, a diver from the high diving board came plunging down directly on top of her. Caught quite unawares she was knocked unconscious and almost drowned before an attendant dived in to rescue her.

After this Jeanette simply couldn't bring herself to enter the water. She only had to look at the green depths of the baths or the greeny blue of the sea, to experience the whole dreadful sensation of drowning all over again. Her parents hoped that one day she would outgrow this fear, but they never forced her to try.

One of Jeanette's favourite pastimes was helping her mother to train the sea lions, Susie and Sammy. These two creatures were treated more or less like members of the family.

Each day they would push their way up the short flight of steps to the caravan and bark like dogs for fishy tit-bits.

"Up! Up!" Jeanette's mother would say and the sea lions, deftly using their flippers, would manoeuvre themselves on to two, small stools and bark again for fish.

After they had had their fish, Jeanette would place on the table a selection of coloured balls; black, green, yellow, white and blue and then the 'game' would start.

"Susie!" Mother would say, "Fetch me the RED ball."

Susie would nuzzle her whiskered face against the coloured balls and immediately pick out, as instructed, the red ball.

"Bravo!" Jeanette would say and Susie clapped her flippers.

Next it would be Sammy's turn and he would sit upright on the stool, alert to join the game.

"Sammy, fetch me the YELLOW ball. The YELLOW ball!"

Again the whiskered face would nuzzle the balls, Sammy would select the yellow one and pass it to Jeanette.

This was not the only trick the sea lions knew, for in the pool outside they were taught new tricks daily; sliding down shoots, leaping through rings,

already numb from the icy water, but she steadily struck out towards her goal. At last she was only a few feet away from the sea lion.

"Sammy! Sammy!" she gasped.

The sea lion raised his head, barked and then swam in a circle around her.

"Let's get the balls, Sammy," gasped Jeanette. "The red one, Sammy. Let's get the red ball. Come along now."

Sammy swam a little nearer.

"Come along, Sammy. Let's get the balls!"

At last he came within reach and Jeanette put her arm around his slippery neck.

"Come on, Sammy, come on, let's go and get the balls."

With her arm still around his neck Jeanette struck out for the shore, but it was cold. Terribly cold.

Jeanette's legs felt just like pieces of lead trailing behind her. Her arms were numb, too, and she was losing her grip on Sammy. But then, as though from nowhere, Jeanette was conscious of voices and the gentle swish of oars. She was conscious, too, of strong hands pulling her aboard a rowing boat—and then nothing.

blowing tunes on a horn, and playing a kind of water polo.

Jeanette was very attached to the sea lions and they to her. They would follow her about, shuffle towards her when she called them by name and always greet her with a series of excitable yelps and barks. In fact, Jeanette found it difficult to imagine life without Sammy and Susie as part of the daily routine.

ONE morning in late October, Jeanette's parents went on a shopping expedition to the city. Jeanette decided to stay behind and go through a few exercises on the trapeze.

Oh, it was a wonderful sensation to fly through the air like a bird, from one trapeze bar to another. Up—down—twist—turn. Up—down—twist and turn. This went on for about fifteen minutes until Jeanette became aware that one of the circus hands was in the ring calling her name.

"Jeanette! Miss Jeanette!"

Jeanette slowed the trapeze and swung herself on to the rope, sliding down in expert fashion.

"Miss Jeanette, it's Sammy! He's gone!"

"Gone!" gasped Jeanette. "What d'you mean by gone?"

"He's gone from the pool, Miss!"

Jeanette, followed by the circus hand, ran out of the marquee and down to the sea lions' pool, and there,

plain to all, was a gap in the protection rails. Someone had probably damaged them during the night and now only Susie swam around in the pool.

She turned to the circus hand. "He'll have gone down to the sea! Let's go and find him, quickly! It's only ten minutes away."

A feeling of dismay clutched Jeanette's heart, for who would be about in the early hours of the morning at this quiet seaside resort to witness the astonishing sight of a sea lion wending his way towards the beach.

Sammy was probably way out to sea by now and lost forever to Jeanette and Susie.

JEANETTE gazed desperately out to sea searching frantically for a sign of Sammy. "There he is! Look!" she cried. She could see a dark, dog-like head bobbing up and down in the calm waters of the tiny bay.

"Sammy! Sammy!" she called, but the sea lion, aware of the call of the open sea, took no heed.

Jeanette started to take her shoes off.

"No, Miss, don't," urged the circus hand.

"Just try and stop me! I must get Sammy back," said Jeanette pulling off her shoes and wading into the cold waters of the bay.

Jeanette struck out towards Sammy, using the fastest stroke she knew, the crawl.

On and on she went, her legs

WHEN Jeanette opened her eyes it was to gaze in bewilderment at the gaily painted walls of the caravan and her mother smiling down at her.

In a dazed manner she looked around again to see Susie and Sammy sitting on their stools beside her bed. They clapped their flippers and nuzzled their whiskered faces about the bedside table, as though they were seeking their coloured balls.

Coloured balls! That was it. Jeanette suddenly remembered what had happened and she struggled to a sitting position.

Her mother squeezed her hand and smiled again. "It's all right! Sammy's back and you're back and everything's going to be all right."

Jeanette leaned back on her pillows and closed her eyes. And then all at once realisation dawned upon her and she sat bolt upright.

"Mother! I've been in the water! I can swim again and I never thought about it at all."

Her mother and father exchanged happy smiles, for they knew that this itself was the greatest reward Jeanette could receive for saving Sammy.

There was a sudden babble of voices and Sammy joined in with a few deep barks as though he knew exactly what it was all about. Perhaps he was thinking how grand it had been in the bay, or perhaps he was thinking how good it was to be back home where there was plenty of coloured balls and always bucketfuls of fish by the sink. Who knows?

Rosie's "HIT" PARADE
S'FUNNY—IT'S TURNED WET ALL OF A SUDDEN.
Raindrops Keep Falling on My Head
In the Good Old Summertime
She Loves You
SHE REALLY DOES, YOU KNOW—IT'S JUST SHE'S GOT A FUNNY WAY OF SHOWING IT!
I Know Where I'm Going
BUT WOLFIE DOESN'T, DOES HE, READERS?
And, of course, Wolfie's favourite—
HELP!

Belle of the Beach

– Or how to stay cool calm and collected when all around are sunburnt and sore.

Start by buying a cheap floppy straw sun hat with a bright design on it. If it's not bright enough for your taste – paint'your own designs on it with shoe paint! A sun hat will not only prevent your hair from drying up but will also protect your face from the sun.

There are several new designs about for swimming caps which look very pretty. One is made like a wig, another like dozens of small, brightly coloured petals, joined together.

Modern brands of sun oil and cream are expensive but worth every penny. Those girls with sensitive skin can buy a cream with a built in protector.

If you tan easily then an oil is for you. There are many brands on the market but why not make your own? One portion of vinegar to three of olive oil makes a very effective sun tan lotion. Shake up well, though!

Take nice fresh salads and pieces of cold roast chicken with you to the beach. They're easy to prepare and good for you.

A crusty loaf, cut and buttered before you leave home is a must. The best containers for the beach are plastic ones with close-fitting, air-tight lids.

If you get thirsty then a very refreshing drink is orange squash mixed with fizzy drink. Allow the drink to cool in the fridge and then keep in a vacuum flask.

The ideal bag for the beach is a plastic one with a large bold design to match your outfit. They can be bought in any large store.

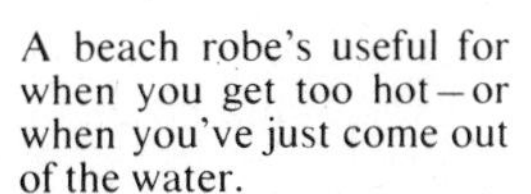

A beach robe's useful for when you get too hot – or when you've just come out of the water.

Made of towelling, they're easy to make and can match your swimming costume.

Buy a bright beach towel in a gay design to match your dress. But make sure it's large. Nothing is more irritating and clingy than sand.

MIRANDA'S MEXICAN BALLET

Later, as the girls arrived at their hotel in the small town of Sierra Pato.
OH, NO! THAT BOY'S WALKING INTO THE PATH OF THAT ONCOMING CAR. I MUST STOP HIM.

Miranda used all her ballet skill and made a tremendous leap, knocking the boy backwards out of the way of the car.

YOU SAVE PANCHO'S LIFE— HOW CAN I EVER REPAY YOU!
I DON'T WANT TO BE REPAID! JUST BE MORE CAREFUL IN FUTURE. DON'T STEP OUT FROM BEHIND PARKED CARS OR BUSES.

The next morning the company went out to see the ancient Aztec temple where they were to perform their ballet.
WHAT A MARVELLOUS BACKGROUND FOR OUR BALLET.

That evening, under floodlights, the performance began with Miranda dancing the lead.

Suddenly the music was stopped by a thunderous roar! Down the mountainside rolled a massive boulder which crunched to a halt only feet from the stage!

Then a loud voice boomed down from the mountainside . . .
YOU HAVE ANGERED THE MOUNTAIN GODS. GO! GO!
The audience panicked and fled from the scene. It was decided to end the evening's performance.

THIS PART OF THE COUNTRY IS STEEPED IN AZTEC TRADITION AND SUPERSTITION, YOU KNOW. STILL, WE'LL TRY AGAIN HERE TOMORROW NIGHT.

Later, at the hotel, Miranda couldn't sleep.
IT'S SO WARM. THINK I'LL GO FOR A STROLL.

Soon . . .
I'M GOING BACK TO THE AZTEC TEMPLE. THERE'S SOMETHING FUNNY ABOUT ALL THIS MOUNTAIN GOD BUSINESS.

OOH! THE MOONLIGHT MAKES EVERYTHING LOOK QUITE CREEPY!

Suddenly out of a secret cave in the pyramid . . .
GOSH—AZTECS! AND WHAT SUPER COSTUMES THEY'RE WEARING!

Miranda's heart beat faster as she edged forward to get a closer view . . .
OH, NO! I'VE KICKED A STONE. THEY'RE BOUND TO HEAR IT.

They did and in no time Miranda was discovered and tied up.
I MUST BE DREAMING! WHAT ARE THEY GOING TO DO WITH ME?

Then the natives began to dance wildly in front of Miranda.
Meanwhile a figure was creeping up behind her . . .

To her surprise the Aztec cut her loose.
NOW FOLLOW ME INTO THE SHADOWS—BUT BE QUICK!

As they ran off, the Aztecs heard them and were soon pounding after them.
OH, THEY'LL CATCH UP WITH US! I KNOW THEY WILL!
HURRY! SAVE YOUR BREATH FOR RUNNING!

They managed to get safely back to the hotel.
AH, NOW I CAN GET RID OF THIS MASK!
OH, WHO CAN HE BE?

WHY IT'S YOU—THE BOY I SAVED FROM BEING RUN OVER BY THE CAR. TELL ME, WHAT WERE THOSE NATIVES DOING AT THE TEMPLE?

THEY ARE REALLY HARMLESS PEOPLE. ALL THEY WISH IS TO KEEP THE ANCIENT AZTEC CITY. IT IS IN BAD SHAPE AND THERE'S NO MONEY TO RESTORE IT. THEY WERE GOING TO MAKE YOU TAKE PART IN TONIGHT'S RITUAL JUST TO SCARE YOU AND YOUR BALLET GIRLS OFF.
The superstitious villagers looked on the Aztec ruins as their very own sacred place and did not welcome outsiders.

WELL I'M GOING TO SEE THE POLICE ABOUT ALL THIS.
NO, NO! YOU MUST NOT GO! PLEASE!

At the police station Miranda told her story to the commissioner.
DO NOT WORRY. WE WILL ROUND UP ALL THE VILLAGERS CONCERNED.

Next morning they were rounded up by the police.
THEY WILL HATE YOU FOR THIS, MIRANDA.
JUST YOU WAIT AND SEE...

Miranda brought the rest of the ballet company down to the police station and then....
PLEASE, LISTEN. WE DO NOT WISH YOU ANY HARM. WE HAVE A PLAN THAT CAN HELP ALL OF YOU AND YOUR AZTEC TEMPLE.

Miranda prepared a special ballet all about the ancient Aztecs. People flocked for miles to see Miranda's ballet and money poured in enabling the people of Sierra Pato to live in comfort and preserve their Aztec temple.

ALL PRESENT AND CORRECT

Choosing presents and wrapping them up can be a pretty boring job. Here are a few tips to brighten things up when it comes to present time!

Be imaginative when wrapping gifts. Wrap one present in wall-paper and make a rosette out of self-adhesive ribbon (they tell you how to do this on the packet). Make another like a Christmas cracker, by wrapping it in crepe paper, tying the ends and then cutting them. Stick shapes of flowers on to the crepe paper.

An interesting and fairly cheap novelty present is a mini swinger. The gentle clicking made by the metal balls is very soothing.

You can make a bottle look like a little figure by adding a hat and a crepe paper cloak. Cut-out shapes for eyes and mouth and a paper scarf complete the look! Another super decoration can be made out of paper petals.

Sponges come in different shapes and make amusing and useful gifts.

A funny present for a friend is a furry insect toy – Uuughh!!

A cheaper present can be small coloured balls of cotton wool in decorative jars. Very useful too.

Slightly more expensive presents are big fluffy brightly coloured powder puffs, but they add that little touch of luxury at bathtime.

This unusual present is a letter rack shaped like a dog. The letters fit into his backbone!

LUCY AND THE DOG NEXT DOOR

Once in bed Lucy looked at her scrapbook of newspaper cuttings and photographs of her champion Beagle, Larry, who had won prizes at Dog Shows throughout the country.

Next morning at breakfast . . .
WHO OWNS THE DOG NEXT DOOR, AUNT LENA?
DOG? THERE'S NO SUCH ANIMAL NEXT DOOR, CHILD. I WOULD CERTAINLY KNOW IF THERE WAS ONE.

WELL I DIDN'T JUST IMAGINE WHAT I SAW LAST NIGHT. PERHAPS THE HOUSE NEXT DOOR NEEDS WATCHING.

The following afternoon while Lucy cleared the garden path of snow, she overheard the two men she'd seen the night before . . .
YOU IDIOT! THAT DOG NEARLY GOT OUT JUST NOW. TIE HIM UP PROPERLY, WE DON'T WANT ANYONE TO SEE HIM.
HMM! NO ONE WOULD SUSPECT ANYTHING EVEN IF THEY DID SEE HIM. HE COULD BE ANY DOG.

I KNEW THERE WAS SOMETHING FISHY GOING ON NEXT DOOR WITH THAT DOG. STILL I CAN'T PROVE IT TO ANYONE.

That night Lucy saw her chance . . .
THE TWO MEN HAVE LEFT IN THEIR VAN. I THINK I'LL GO ROUND AND SEE IF THE DOG'S ALL RIGHT. I WOULDN'T BE SURPRISED IF THEY WEREN'T FEEDING HIM.

Soon . .
WELL, HERE GOES!

In no time Lucy came across the Beagle.
OH, I WAS RIGHT! YOU POOR THING. YOU'VE NEITHER FOOD NOR WATER.

LET'S SEE YOUR COLLAR—HMM, YOUR NAME IS SANDY. I SEEM TO REMEMBER A BEAGLE CALLED SANDY, BUT MAYBE I'M MISTAKEN. COME ON, BOY, I'M NOT LEAVING YOU HERE TO THE MERCY OF THESE THUGS.

Sandy happily followed Lucy back to Great Aunt Lena's house.

After a good feed in the kitchen Lucy took Sandy up to her bedroom.
YOU JUST SIT THERE, SANDY. I'M GOING TO HAVE A LOOK THROUGH MY SCRAP-BOOK.

Suddenly Lucy found it . . .
I KNEW I'D HEARD YOUR NAME BEFORE,BOY. YOU'VE BEEN SECOND AND THIRD TO LARRY IN A COUPLE OF DOG SHOWS. THOSE MEN MUST HAVE STOLEN YOU. NEVER MIND, YOU'RE SAFE NOW! I'LL PHONE THE POLICE IN THE MORNING.

But Lucy had not slept for long when . . .
SOMEONE'S SCREAMING! GREAT AUNT LENA MUST BE IN TROUBLE.

As soon as Lucy opened the bedroom door Sandy raced past her.

Meanwhile in Great Aunt Lena's bedroom . . .
WHERE'S THE DOG? WE KNOW HE'S HERE SOMEWHERE. WE FOLLOWED THE FOOTPRINTS THROUGH THE SNOW FROM NEXT DOOR.
THERE'S NO ANIMAL IN THIS HOUSE. GO AWAY OR I'LL PHONE THE POLICE!

Sandy burst into Great Aunt Lena's room . . .
THERE HE IS—GET A HOLD OF HIM, LEN.
AGH! IT'S A DOG!
YOU DO, MATE, I DON'T FANCY THESE TEETH. HE HASN'T FORGOTTEN HOW YOU KICKED HIM.
The two thugs were scared to move an inch.
QUICK, LUCY, PHONE THE POLICE. WHAT A MARVELLOUS DOG—HOLDING OFF THESE VILLAINS SO BRAVELY!

In no time at all the police arrived.
YOU DID WELL, LASS. THIS DOG'S BEEN MISSING FOR A WEEK AND THE OWNERS HAVE BEEN FRANTIC ABOUT HIM. I TRUST YOU'LL BE ABLE TO KEEP YOUR EYE ON SANDY UNTIL THEY CAN CALL AND COLLECT HIM.

WELL ONLY IF...
OF COURSE I DON'T MIND, LUCY. AFTER THE CLEVER ANIMAL SAVING MY LIFE—HMM. DON'T KNOW WHY I EVER DISLIKED DOGS REALLY!

The next morning Sandy and Lucy had great fun.

Then Sandy's owners came to collect him.
WE CAN'T THANK YOU ENOUGH, LUCY AND I HOPE YOU'LL ACCEPT THIS CHEQUE FROM US AS A REWARD.
WHY THANK YOU, MR FORBES.
BUT OH, DEAR, THREE WEEKS LEFT WITH GREAT AUNT LENA AND NO SANDY TO PLAY WITH NOW.

But that evening Lucy got the happiest surprise of her life.
WHY—IT'S LARRY!
YES, DEAR. I HAD HIM SENT OVER FROM THE KENNELS.AFTER SEEING HOW HAPPY YOU WERE WITH SANDY.I KNEW YOU'D NEED LARRY'S COMPANY FOR THE REST OF THE HOLIDAYS. I'M A BIT TOO OLD FOR CHASING STICKS IN THE PARK!

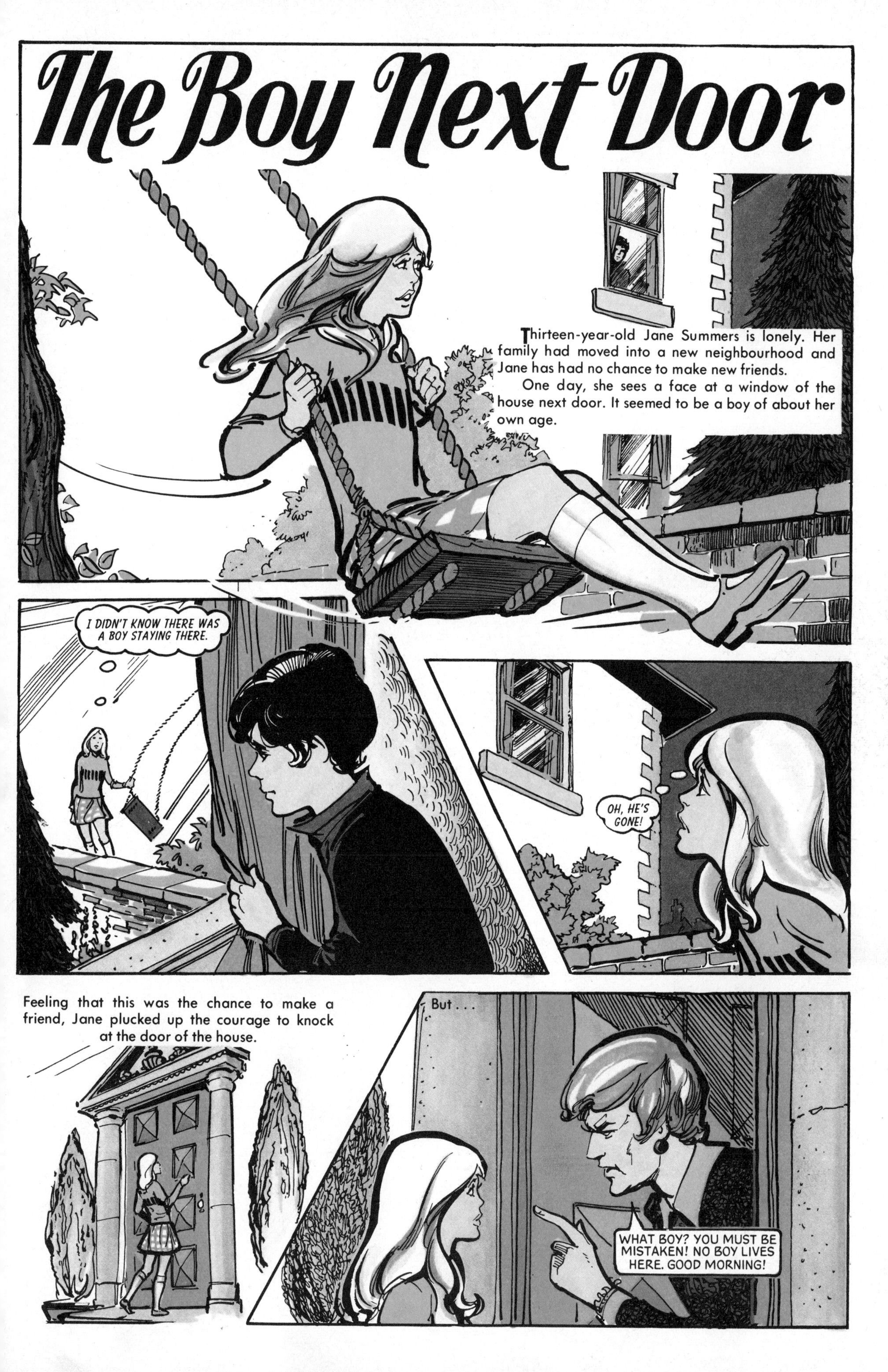
The Boy Next Door
Thirteen-year-old Jane Summers is lonely. Her family had moved into a new neighbourhood and Jane has had no chance to make new friends.
One day, she sees a face at a window of the house next door. It seemed to be a boy of about her own age.
I DIDN'T KNOW THERE WAS A BOY STAYING THERE.
OH, HE'S GONE!
Feeling that this was the chance to make a friend, Jane plucked up the courage to knock at the door of the house.
But . . .
WHAT BOY? YOU MUST BE MISTAKEN! NO BOY LIVES HERE. GOOD MORNING!

When Jane returned to her own garden, the severe-looking woman was pulling the heavy curtains across the window.
I'M SURE I SAW A BOY! I COULDN'T HAVE DREAMT IT. MAYBE BECAUSE I'VE NO CHUMS I JUST WILLED SOMEONE TO BE AT THE WINDOW.
Later, Jane paid a visit to the public park.
Suddenly she took a tumble.
OUCH!
A girl who happened to be nearby came to Jane's aid. She said her name was Trudi.
IT WAS SILLY OF ME TO FALL. I WAS DAY-DREAMING ABOUT A BOY I SAW THIS MORNING—AT LEAST I THINK I SAW HIM...
Trudi walked home with Jane who told her what had happened that morning.
HERE'S THE HOUSE I WAS TELLING YOU ABOUT.
AND LOOK! THERE'S THE BOY! I WASN'T DREAMING!

But, by the time Trudi looked up, the face had disappeared.
I'LL TAKE YOU TO THE YOUTH CLUB TONIGHT, JANE, AND YOU CAN MEET SOME OF MY FRIENDS.
OK! THANKS, TRUDI!
So, that night—
THIS IS GREAT, BUT I CAN'T STAY LONG. I HAVE TO BE HOME BY NINE.
On the way home—
I STILL CAN'T GET THAT BOY OUT OF MY MIND!
As she reached the mystery house—
THERE HE IS.
Jane waved, and the boy waved back
I'M DEFINITELY NOT IMAGINING THIS!

In her own house, Jane overheard a snatch of a conversation between her parents.
I SAW THOSE STRANGE NEIGHBOURS OF OURS DRIVE AWAY IN THEIR CAR TONIGHT.
She slipped out and knocked at the door of the house, hoping the boy would answer.
NO ANSWER.
Jane found a window slightly open.
I'M GOING TO FIND OUT WHAT'S HAPPENING HERE. MAYBE THEY'VE KIDNAPPED THAT BOY OR SOMETHING.
She was a bit scared as she tiptoed up the stairs.
Finding a door with a light showing beneath, she tapped lightly.
IT'S ME—THE GIRL FROM NEXT DOOR. ARE YOU THERE?
PLEASE GO AWAY! I HEAR THE CAR COMING. YOU'RE ONLY MAKING ME MORE UNHAPPY! I WON'T COME TO THE WINDOW AGAIN!
Jane just managed to get out of the window as the car drew up outside.

Jane watched the woman and a man enter the house.
YOU'RE SURE THAT GIRL DIDN'T SEE HIM? IT COULD BE DANGEROUS. WE MIGHT HAVE TO MOVE HOUSE!
THAT BOY HAS BEEN KIDNAPPED. I'M GOING TO THE POLICE!
She raced out into the street, waved down a police car and panted out her story.
GOOD EVENING, MADAM. WE'RE CALLING TO MAKE ENQUIRIES ABOUT A BOY THIS GIRL SAYS SHE SAW IN THIS HOUSE.
The woman burst into tears.
IT'S NO GOOD, STEFAN! WE ARE DISCOVERED! BRING THE BOY DOWN!
PETER!

AUNT KIRSTY! DON'T CRY! IT COULDN'T GO ON FOREVER!
AUNT KIRSTY! OH, DEAR! I'VE BOOBED!
The man, Stefan, explained that young Peter's parents had been killed in an uprising in a certain European country. Peter had been smuggled into Britain
OH, I'M SORRY! I'VE RUINED EVERYTHING!
LEAVE IT TO US, LASS. WE'LL MAKE OUR REPORT AND SEE WHAT HAPPENS.
Some weeks later, Jane was waiting outside her house, very excited.
HERE THEY COME!
The car drew up and Peter bounded out.
I CAN STAY! I CAN STAY! YOUR POLICE ARE VERY KIND! NOW I CAN LIVE LIKE AN ORDINARY BOY AGAIN!
And Peter started his normal life right away—off he went with Jane, Trudi and their other friends.
HE IS IN NO DANGER NOW, KIRSTY. THANKS TO THE GIRL FROM NEXT DOOR!

Words and Music

A selection of scenes from famous film musicals which are based on well-known books or plays.

Mark Lester asking for more in "Oliver!" adapted from Charles Dickens' famous novel "Oliver Twist".

A scene from "My Fair Lady", the musical based on George Bernard Shaw's "Pygmalion".

The scene here is from "West Side Story", a modern day version of Shakespeare's tender love story "Romeo and Juliet".

Another film based on the works of Charles Dickens. This time it's "Scrooge" from the book, "A Christmas Carol".

WHEN VINEGAR LIL TURNED PURPLE

FROM SALLY DAY'S CASEBOOK

Pupils at Benstead School hold their own court proceedings. Sally Day is Clerk of the Court and with Head girl Alison Wylie as judge they have their own counsels and jury to mete out justice.

I THINK I've mentioned before that when it comes to plotting and planning, Dodie Smith takes the biscuit. But during this little fracas we all thought she'd come unstuck!

It all began when Maud Jackson appeared in court a week or so ago . . .

"You were discovered talking to a male pupil when you should have been in class," quoth prosecuting counsel Susan Jacobs. "How do you plead?"

"Guilty," said Maud. "We were discussing our homework!"

Someone giggled and Alison Wylie rapped with her gavel.

"This is not a matter for levity," she said sternly, skipping lessons is a very serious offence . . .!"

'Vinegar Lil' or Miss Drewitt had been on the warpath again. As you know, apart from taking us for Maths and History she is very sour!

So, natch, when Ye Olde Schoole went comprehensive, and we had lashings of groovy fellers dropped right into our laps, we thought the balloon would probably go up.

Vin Lil staggered round under the new regime for a few days, looking sort of stunned like someone had struck her behind the ear with a stuffed sock. We were a bit cagey about the male species ourselves at first, keeping to one side of the playground during break, indulging in our usual maidenly pursuits such as chatting about gear, filing our nails etcet, while the manly art of football was played on the other.

We knew Vin Lil, you see, and wanted to see which way the cat would jump (as the saying goes) but when she made no move, we began to mingle.

"Super!" said Maud Jackson, "there's plenty to go round. There'll be a bloke for everyone!"

"E-even me?" quavered Podge.

Maud studied her.

"Stranger things have happened," she said. "Nature's funny y'know!"

"Don't be downhearted, Podge," I said. "Some boys LIKE fat girls."

Podge clenched her fists.

"I'm not going to be beaten this time," she said. "I'll get a feller of my very own if it kills me. I'm going to get a book out of the library."

With which dark threat she toddled off.

Well . . . that was Tuesday, and by Wednesday afternoon, Podge had a round bloke chasing her every break, dinnertime—in fact whenever she hove into the horizon. Despite her poundage, Podge can put on a fair turn of speed when required, but by Thursday he'd met her down by the school dustbins and Romance with a capital 'Ah-h!' had set in for Podge.

I was curious how Podge had done it. Had she, (I enquired) gone to the local bookworm basement or was it her natural charms that had worked the miracle? Had she found some encyclopaedia on how to attract blokes or was it just 'like calling to like' i.e. both of them being pork pie addicts?

"If you'd shut up," quoth Podge rudely, "I might tell you."

She handed me a crumpled paperback entitled 'How To Get Your Man' and I studied it for a minute.

"You fathead!" I said, pointing to the small print. "This is a book of rules for the Canadian Mounted Police!"

"It worked, didn't it?" said Podge. "I only read the summing-up on the last page. It just says 'Keep Running!'"

And that was all Podge had done! But it was too good to last. Vin Lil was coming out of her coma and was soon harrassing couples in the playground and going round with a mine detector and a set expression trying to keep the girls well away from the boys.

"I thought this would happen," said Dodie. "We'll have to think of something . . ."

We operated a system for a day or so, taking it in turns to keep an eye on Lil and give the warning when she was in the offing. But it didn't work.

She caught Maud Jackson and Danny Platt comparing notes when they should have been at maths and the fat was well and truly in the fire!

The jury found them guilty and gave them ten days in detention without the option.

WHEN we turned up at school the following Monday, we could see straight off that Vin Lil had been busy with a paint brush over the weekend. There was a whacking white line right down the middle of the playground with 'BOYS' written in one half and 'GIRLS' in the other!

The Hall had been divided as well, the white line running right up the walls and along the ceiling just in case anyone thought of getting together round the chandeliers. Vin Lil was smirking away on all cylinders as Miss Waring told us what it was all about.

"It's a wonder they didn't use barbed wire," whispered Dodie. "At least we'll be all right in the classrooms!"

But, they had been treated as well, and life looked grim!

"It's more like a prison than a school!" gritted Dodie at break-time. "What d'you bet that next term's uniform will be something snappy in grey with arrows on it?"

"Vin Lil's trying to ruin the whole system," I said. "Before long she'll have the blokes out of Benstead altogether."

"No, she won't!" snapped Dodie, "because I've got a PLAN. Follow me, you two!"

When she showed us a notice on the school board we had to admit that her present one looked like a winner. It read: OPTIONS FOR THE TERM'S WORK. PUPILS MAY SELECT SUBJECTS FROM THE FOLLOWING:— There was a list a mile long and Dodie pointed to two little items at the bottom—Woodwork and Needlework.

"They can keep us apart in the ordinary lessons, but not in these two. You remember what was said about equal opportunity for girls? Well, I vote the three of us PLUMP FOR WOODWORK THIS TERM!"

"Gosh!" I said, for want of a better word.

"You've said it!" said Dodie.

★★★★★

The trouble was that our plan must have leaked, because not only Podge, me, and Dodie turned up for woodwork next session but all the rest of the girls in Form Four as well! What was even worse was that there wasn't a bloke in sight!

The woodwork master, a friendly old soul with specs and a leather apron, was a bit cut up about it at first and beetled off to find where the male members of his class had got to. He discovered them in the Needlework Room, of all places, muttering into their collars while they embroidered flowered aprons and table runners.

"You fathead!" I told Dodie as I wrestled with the tea-tray I was making. "Now we're lumbered with this for the rest of the term—and no blokes!"

But she wasn't listening, being busy binding up Podge's thumb where she'd hit it with a hammer.

For the next few woodwork lessons we struggled on, and Dodie got more and more unpopular. I'd had several stabs (literally!) at making the joints at the edge of my tea-tray and each time the little old woodwork master sawed them off and told me to start again.

"By the time you've finished that tray," he told me, looking over the top of his specs, "it'll be about big enough to hold half a bun!"

And he tottered off, shaking his head as if he didn't know what things were coming to.

That was the day the chisel slipped and I went home in splints. Most of the girls were a bit chipped by this time, and Ye Parents began to complain.

And it wasn't only the girls' parents who were complaining. Spike Watson's mum—a hefty number in a hair-net—came up to the school waving her umbrella and complaining that they were turning her lad into a sissy.

"The neighbours are talking about his homework—sitting there for everyone to see, doing his KNITTING!" she stormed. "If this is what you call comprehensive education, you can KEEP it!"

This about summed up the feelings of all the nearests and dearests, and when squads of them began collecting regularly outside the gates, Miss Waring began to get panicky.

"A special session of the school court will be convened," she told us in hall, "to try the whole matter of our new system of education. Parents will be present . . ."

Vin Lil was grinning away at the back of the hall.

"Now you've done it!" I complained to Dodie. "Before we know where we are the blokes'll be out of Benstead and we'll be back to our single state!"

★★★★★

"THE charge brought by the parents," said Alison, sitting as judge, "is that the present system is producing girlish boys and boyish girls. The accused, in this case, is the SYSTEM. Evidence will be presented for and against in the usual manner."

It seemed funny, no one being in the dock I mean, and I was kept pretty busy as several parents gave evidence but when Vin Lil took the stand I thought everything was up.

"I said from the first that the system wouldn't work!" she shrilled. "To put boys and gels together in this fashion is little short of DISgusting!"

Dodie was handling the defence and up to then hadn't said much. But now she had Vin Lil in the dock she went into action.

"Why didn't you think the system would work, Miss Drewitt?" she asked politely.

"What I thought doesn't matter," she smirked. "The results speak for themselves!"

"You mean that the girls and boys being in close contact was bound to produce such results?"

"Of course!"

Dodie shuffled her notes, then looked up.

"But surely there has been no close contact between the two? Isn't it true that the boys have been rigidly separated from the girls?" She pointed to that big, white line. "Haven't all the rooms in the school been treated in this way to keep them apart?"

Vin Lil stuttered.

"Impertinence—!"

"Answer the question, please," ruled Alison quietly.

Lil gulped.

"Well—yes, I suppose so."

Dodie took a turn in front of the box.

"Isn't it a fact, then, that the results that have been shown to the court have, in fact, been produced BECAUSE of separation . . .?"

Vin Lil went purple, but didn't answer.

Dodie rested her case and the jury gave its verdict in favour of the system, with a recommendation that the white lines be removed forthwith and pupils allowed to mingle freely!

★★★★★

When everybody had gone, I helped Dodie out of her gown.

"Gosh," I said, "we had you all wrong, Dodie. But you were lucky the way things turned out . . ."

"Lucky nothing!" she snapped. "I leaked our plan about woodwork to the rest of the girls and I dropped a word in the ear of my bloke that he might like to try needlework."

"You mean you planned it this way all along?" I breathed admiringly. "Parents and—and everything?"

"Everything," she said. "You lot should have a little more faith, that's what!"

And she stalked out, complete with biscuit.

See you!

PERFECT

Here are eight famous partnerships, past and present, who have thrilled show-jumping audiences all over the world.

Anneli Drummond-Hay and 'Merely-A-Monarch'.

Lt.-Col. Harry Llewellyn and 'Foxhunter'.

Pat Koechlin-Smythe and 'Flanagan'.

Captain P. D'Inzeo and 'The Rock'.

PARTNERS

Harvey Smith and 'O'Malley'.

Marion Coakes-Mould and 'Stroller'.

Peter Robeson and 'Firecrest'.

David Broome and 'Mr Softee'.

PATTI'S PONY EXPRESS

IT'S the year 1865. Thirteen-year-old Patti Forbes lives on her father's small ranch in Arizona.

The Forbes family isn't well-to-do, and Mr Forbes is waiting for a banker's draft from the East for the sale of some cattle.

Their supplies run low as the weeks pass and there's no sign of the money.

Patti had caught and trained the ponies herself and was very attached to them. It was with a heavy heart that she arrived in nearby Robson City to put the horses up for sale.

The mayor of the small town was speaking to the gathering.

The Pony Express which delivered the mail all over the West, was just starting up in their area, and the people of Robson City were disappointed that it wouldn't come to their little town.

WHAT'S ALL THE FUSS ABOUT? YOU DON'T NEED THE PONY EXPRESS! I'LL DELIVER YOUR MAIL FOR YOU!
The men all laughed at Patti.

I'M NOT JOKING! I COULD DO IT STANDING ON MY HEAD! I'LL SHOW YOU!

Patti gave a wonderful exhibition of trick riding.

WELL, SHE SAID SHE COULD DO IT ON HER HEAD!

OK, GIRLIE! WE'RE CONVINCED! YOU'VE EARNED YOUR CHANCE!

A few days later, Patti was in Big Creek, picking up the mail for Robson City.
YOU'RE A MITE YOUNG TO BE DOING THIS JOB!
I'LL BE ALL RIGHT. I'LL BE BACK IN A COUPLE OF DAYS WITH MORE MAIL!
MC LAGLEN HAWKS
STORE
ELAM & BRAN
SERGIO FORD

Soon Patti was out in the wilds, heading for home.
THAT LOOKS LIKE SMOKE SIGNALS!

Then—

The war party attacked.
Patti managed to get slightly ahead of the Indians.

She swung herself up into a tree.

The Indians galloped past below, following her horse.
HERE COMES THE LAST ONE!

I NEED YOUR HORSE, BUDDY!

Patti scrambled on to the Indian's horse.

She managed to avoid the war party and knew that her own pony would find its way home.

But the half-wild Indian horse was a bit of a handful.

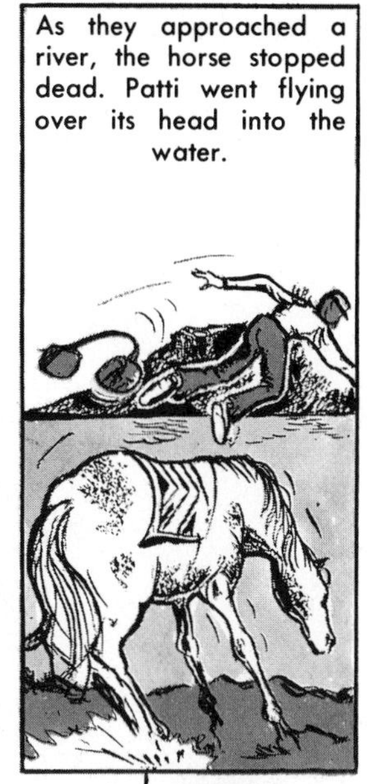
As they approached a river, the horse stopped dead. Patti went flying over its head into the water.

AT LEAST THE MAIL'S NOT WET!
US MAIL

Just then—
HAND OVER THOSE MAIL BAGS!

OOF!
OK! HERE!

THAT SHOT FRIGHTENED MY HORSE...

The man was Jack Kane, a well-known outlaw. He'd been lying in wait for Patti.
SO I'LL NEED YOUR HELP!

Patti "persuaded" Jack to carry her. After a few miles . . .
THAT'S A BIT OF LUCK! THERE'S MY PONY!

Patti had a tremendous reception when she reached Robson City with the mail and Jack in tow.

Jack was locked up, then the Mayor opened the mail-bag.
WHY! THERE'S A THING! THE FIRST LETTER IS FOR YOUR PAW, PATTI!

The letter contained the banker's draft for Mr Forbes.
WELL, YOU'LL BE ABLE TO KEEP YOUR PONIES NOW, PATTI, AND GIVE UP THAT JOB!

I'M NOT GIVING UP MY JOB, PAW! I ENJOY IT TOO MUCH!

SLAVE OF THE ROMANS
LORNA BUTTERWICK is a schoolgirl who is very interested in history—as is her father.
One glorious summer's day, they set out to explore an old Roman road . . .

THIS IS THE OLD ROMAN ROAD, LORNA. JUST IMAGINE—A GENUINE LINK WITH JULIUS CAESAR, 2000 YEARS OLD!
IT'S STRANGE. I'VE NEVER BEEN HERE BEFORE, YET IT SEEMS VERY FAMILIAR.

Her father having gone to explore, Lorna sat on a cairn to enjoy the sun and have a snack.
GOSH, THIS IS A PERFECT PLACE TO SOAK UP THE SUN AND MUNCH IN TO THESE CHEESE SANDWICHES.
Cheese had the strangest effect on Lorna—she felt herself being whisked through time and space away from the mound of stones—

—until she arrived with a bump, and heard the sound of marching feet approaching!

IT—IT CAN'T BE! I MUST BE SEEING THINGS!

IT'S A ROMAN LEGION!

The Legion's tribune spotted Lorna.
HOW DARE YOU STRAY FROM YOUR WORK, BRITON! GUARDS, SEIZE HER!

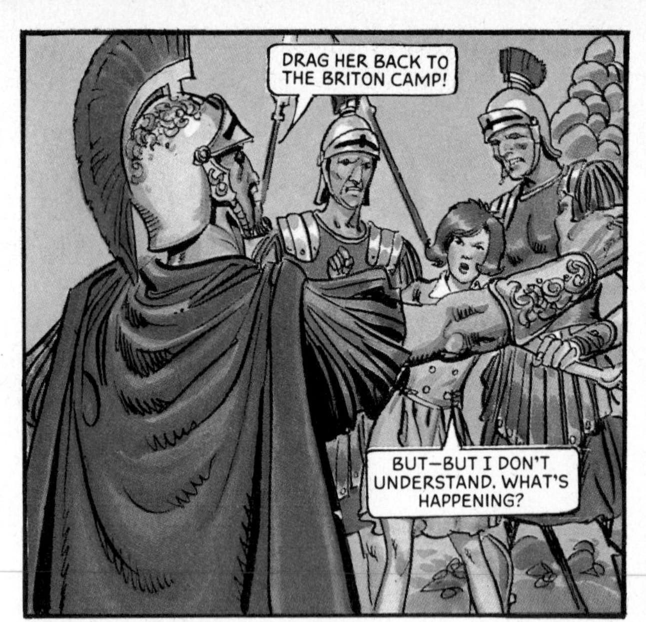
DRAG HER BACK TO THE BRITON CAMP!
BUT—BUT I DON'T UNDERSTAND. WHAT'S HAPPENING?

Despite her protests, Lorna was bundled off to the labour camp.
BACK TO WORK—AND DON'T WANDER OFF AGAIN!

All day, Lorna was forced to work on the road.

Later—
THE TIME HAS COME—WE MUST RID OURSELVES OF THE ROMAN YOKE! WE WILL STRIKE THREE NIGHTS FROM NOW!

GUARD YOUR WORDS, BROTHERS, FOR I FEAR WE MAY BE OVERHEARD BY YON STRANGE GIRL.

I'LL WAGER SHE'S BEEN SENT BY THE ROMANS TO SPY ON US.
YES, SHE'S NOT ONE OF US. LET'S SHOW THE ROMANS WHAT WE THINK OF THEIR SPIES!
PLEASE, LET ME EXPLAIN— I'M REALLY ONE OF YOU...

LIES! LIES! GO BACK TO YOUR ROMAN FRIENDS!
STONE HER! DRIVE HER AWAY!

PHEW! I DON'T KNOW WHAT I DID TO DESERVE THAT. WHAT DO I DO NOW?
DRIVE THESE MUTINOUS BRITONS BACK TO THEIR CAMP!

The Roman tribune sought out Lorna.
THAT GIRL DOES NOT LOOK LIKE A BARBARIC BRITON. I'LL TAKE HER AS A SERVANT.

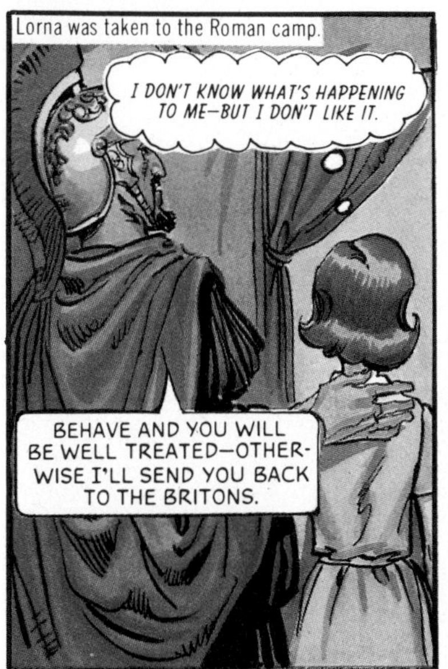
Lorna was taken to the Roman camp.
I DON'T KNOW WHAT'S HAPPENING TO ME—BUT I DON'T LIKE IT.
BEHAVE AND YOU WILL BE WELL TREATED—OTHERWISE I'LL SEND YOU BACK TO THE BRITONS.

Lorna was set to work as the tribune's personal servant.

That night—
THE BRITONS, I FEAR ARE PLANNING A REVOLT. I'D SAY WE OUGHT TO MARCH TONIGHT, CATCH THEM BY SURPRISE AND CRUSH THEM.

Lorna overheard their plan.
AGREED! WE MARCH IN AN HOUR!
THEY'RE PLANNING TO MURDER THEM IN THEIR SLEEP!

She slipped unnoticed from the tent.
I MUST WARN THE BRITONS—AFTER ALL THEY ARE MY ANCESTORS.

WILL I BE IN TIME? THE LEGIONS CANNOT BE FAR BEHIND ME NOW!

When she reached the Britons' camp—
LISTEN TO ME, EVERYBODY! ARM YOURSELVES, THE ROMANS ARE COMING TO ATTACK YOU!
IT'S THE ROMAN SPY AGAIN!

HUH! JUST ANOTHER ROMAN TRICK!
PLEASE BELIEVE ME!

TIE HER UP—WE'LL SHOW HER WHAT WE DO TO ROMAN SPIES!
NO, STOP! YOU MUST LISTEN TO ME!

Minutes later—
WAIT! WAIT!
LIGHT THE FIRE!

LOOK, THE GIRL WAS TELLING THE TRUTH. THOSE ARE ROMAN TORCHES YONDER!

Lorna was cut down from the stake.
LOOK AFTER THE GIRL. WE SHALL REPAY HER WHEN THE BATTLE IS DONE.
ONLY HER BRAVERY HAS SAVED US FROM BEING SLAUGHTERED IN OUR BEDS!

Surprised that the Britons were prepared for the attack, the Romans lost heart and fled.

THE POOR CHILD IS HALF-DEAD. SHE ALMOST GAVE HER LIFE TO SAVE US.
IT WILL NOT BE FORGOTTEN. WE SHALL SEE TO THAT.

Later—
THIS CAIRN WE HAVE BUILT IN HONOUR OF A BRAVE YOUNG GIRL WHO SAVED ALL OUR LIVES. BY THIS SHE SHALL BE REMEMBERED!

Suddenly, Lorna felt her senses reeling—
—as she was once again whisked back through time and space.

LORNA, WAKE UP!
OH, IT WAS JUST A DREAM! IT MUST HAVE BEEN THE CHEESE I ATE.

But when Lorna told her father of her dream—
IT'S HARDLY POSSIBLE, BUT YOU'VE JUST TOLD ME THE HISTORY OF THIS CAIRN—AND THE GIRL'S NAME WAS... LORNA!

BUT PERHAPS YOU'VE HEARD THE STORY BEFORE? COME ON, TIME TO GO HOME.
BUT IF SHE HADN'T HEARD IT BEFORE, THEN HOW......

UP-TO-DATE
KATE
OUR DEDICATED FOLLOWER OF FASHION

Early one morning . . .
AHA! WHAT'S THIS?
MISS 2000 ?
FASHION COMPETITION!
FIRST PRIZE
£100!

DESIGN AND MAKE–UP A FASHION FOR THE YEAR 2000. I SHOULD BE ABLE TO DO THAT.

AND THINK WHAT I COULD DO WITH THAT £100—IT COULD GO TOWARDS AN AFRICAN HOLIDAY... OR SUPER CLOTHES...OR...

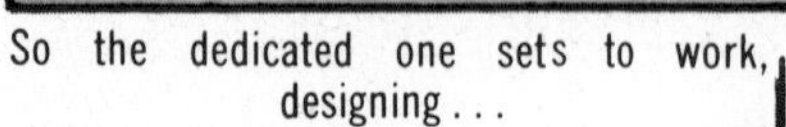
So the dedicated one sets to work, designing . . .

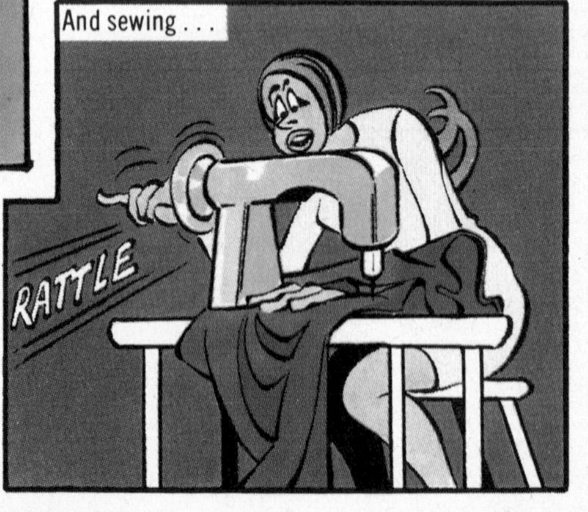
And sewing . . .
RATTLE

Until—
SUPER! THIS OUTFIT'S BOUND TO WIN THE COMPETITION!

The day of the competition—
'BYE, DAD!
GOOD LUCK, KATE!
Shortly—
IS IT?
IT IS!
IT ISN'T!
IT IS! COME ON!

I SAY! YOU ARE THE BOBBY BUBBLES GIRL AND I CLAIM THE £5!
BONG!
Bobby Bubbles

COME ON!
WHAT'S GOING ON?
HEY! YOU ARE THE BOBBY BUBBLES...
...AND I CLAIM MY £5!

THERE SHE IS!
YOU ARE THE...
WHERE'S THE FIVE QUID THEN, DUCKY?
FIVE POUNDS STERLING, THANKING YOU VERY MUCH, KIND MADAM, YES PLEASE?

WHERE IS SHE?
PHEW! ESCAPED AT LAST!
LET ME AT HER!

Then—
SO THAT'S IT! MY OUTFIT'S EXACTLY THE SAME AS HERS!
THE Bobby Bubbles Girl
IN TOWN TODAY. IF YOU HAVE A PACKET OF BOBBY BUBBLES WASHING POWDER YOU CAN CLAIM £5!

I'M GETTING OUT OF THIS GEAR. I DON'T WANT TRAMPLED IN ANOTHER STAMPEDE. BUT I DON'T HAVE TIME TO GO HOME AGAIN BEFORE THE COMPETITION.

When Kate arrived at the competition . . .
HO! HO! YOU WERE MEANT TO DESIGN A COSTUME FOR 2000 A.D., NOT 2000 B.C., M'DEAR!
THESE LEAVES AND THINGS WERE ALL I COULD FIND!

The Pride of St. Petersburg

The Dancing Days of Anna Pavlova

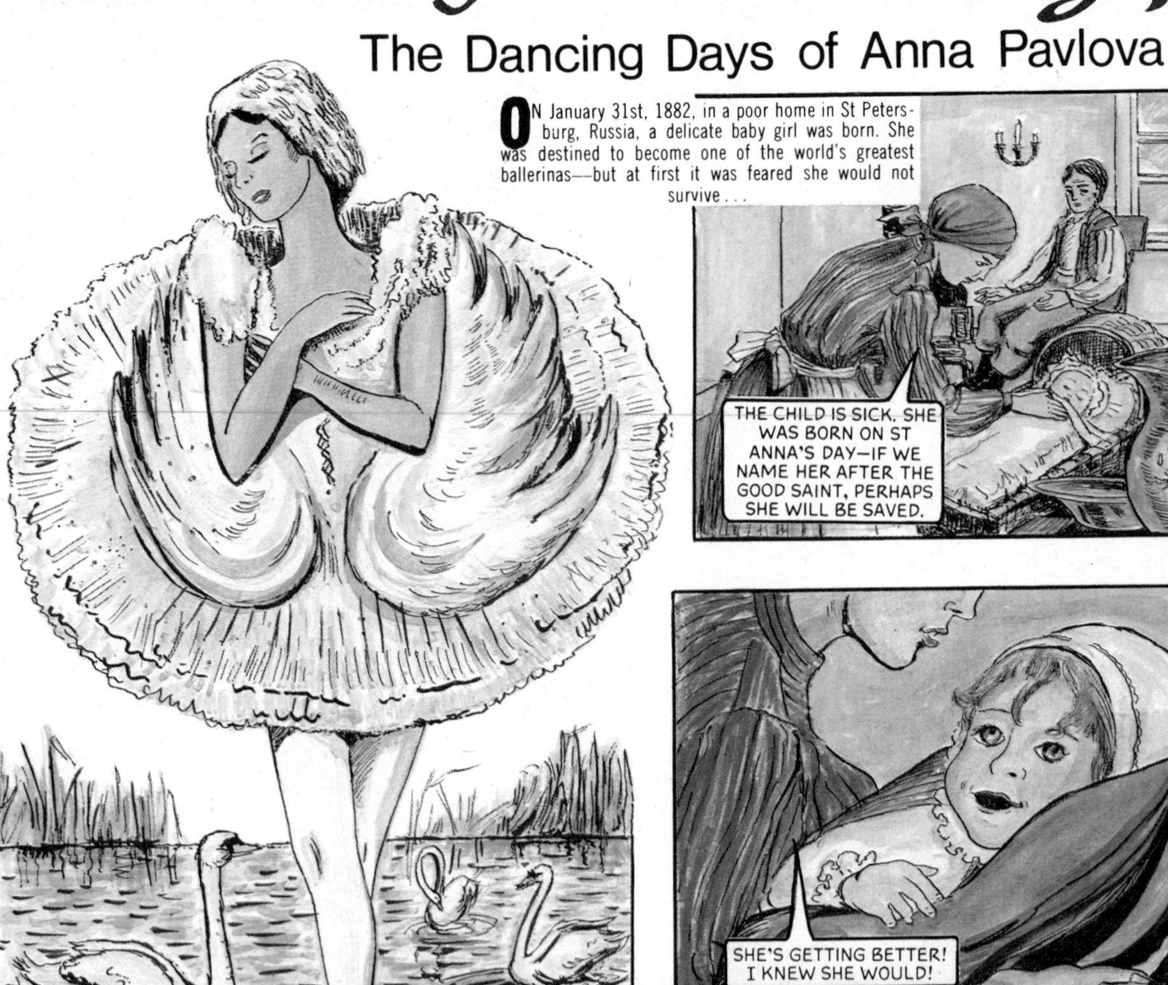

Anna loved the countryside.
HOW LOVELY THE COUNTRYSIDE IS! LOOK, SQUIRREL, I CAN SPRING JUST LIKE YOU.

Anna would imitate all the creatures of the forest—
I MUST BE GRACEFUL AND GLIDE—JUST LIKE A SWAN.

Four years later, Anna prepared to visit her mother in St Petersburg—
YOU HAVE GROWN SO STRONG, YOUR MOTHER WILL HARDLY RECOGNISE YOU!

Madame Pavlova tried to make Anna's visit home a happy one. She took her to the Marvinsky Theatre to see a ballet . . .
IT'S THE MOST BEAUTIFUL THING I'VE EVER SEEN.

MAMA, I'VE MADE UP MY MIND. I MUST BE A DANCER!
IT WON'T BE EASY, CHILD. BUT WE HAVE THE IMPERIAL BALLET SCHOOL IN ST PETERSBURG. WE SHALL PAY IT A VISIT.

But disappointment awaited Anna at the school—
I AM SORRY, MY DEAR, BUT YOU ARE TOO YOUNG. COME BACK WHEN YOU ARE TEN. BUT REMEMBER—THE TEST IS SEVERE.

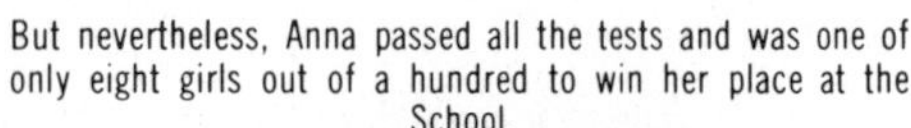
But nevertheless, Anna passed all the tests and was one of only eight girls out of a hundred to win her place at the School.

Anna died suddenly at the Hague in 1931.

A prize is awarded in Paris in memory of her genius—to young dancers who dance with "spirit".

ANNA PAVLOVA

A THIN TIME for TESSA
THIRTEEN-YEAR old Tessa Corridon was rather tubby, and when her mother began discussing holiday plans . . .
YOU'LL NEED A NEW SWIMSUIT, TESSA, AND A TENNIS OUTFIT.
AND WHERE WILL I GET ANYTHING TO FIT ME?

That night Tessa's nightmares rose from memories of the previous year's holiday.
AH, HERE COMES FATTY!
WATCH OUT FOR THE TIDAL WAVE!

I CAN'T AFFORD TO GET ANY TUBBIER.
And while all the other kids wolfed down ice cream, Tessa was forced to refuse it.

Next morning . . .
OH, MUMMY, IT'S JUST NO USE. I'VE DIETED AND DIETED AND LOOK— I'M FATTER THAN EVER!
YOU'VE—ER—GROWN SINCE THAT DRESS WAS MADE, DEAR. YOU MUST DISCIPLINE YOURSELF.

So, at breakfast . . .
BUT, MUM, THIS LEMON JUICE TASTES SO SOUR
DRINK IT UP, TESSA!

Later in the garden . . .
THAT'S THE PHONE RINGING, MUM!
RELAX, MARY WILL ANSWER IT. YOUR TAN'S COMING UP BEAUTIFULLY.
HMM! THE SUN COULD HARDLY MISS ME!

THAT'S YOUR NIECE ON THE PHONE, MA'AM. THEY'RE IN A SPOT OF TROUBLE AT THE FARM.
AREN'T THEY ALWAYS! WHY MY SISTER SHOULD MARRY A FARMER FROM THE BACK OF BEYOND, I CAN'T IMAGINE! YOU SPEAK TO YOUR COUSIN, TESSA!

OH, KATHY, YOU POOR THING. SO THERE'S ONLY YOU LEFT TO COPE. I'LL COME UP THERE AND HELP YOU.
THANKS, TESSA. IT'S VERY GOOD OF YOU.

THERE'S BEEN A CRASH IN THE LAND ROVER! AUNT MURIEL'S BROKEN HER LEG, MUM, AND UNCLE CLIFF'S IN HOSPITAL. I MUST GO AND HELP KATHY.
BUT WHAT CAN YOU DO, DEAR? LOOK, LET ME SEND KATHY SOME MONEY INSTEAD.
IT'S NOT MONEY SHE NEEDS. IT'S HELP!
OH, WELL, IF YOU'RE DETERMINED. BUT YOU MUST REMEMBER TO STICK TO YOUR DIET.

Meanwhile at Forest Heights. Farm . . .
SHE'LL HAVE TO WORK OR STARVE HERE—THAT'S THE RULE!

The following day, as Tessa stepped out of an ancient taxi—
I WOULDN'T HAVE HIRED YOU IF I'D KNOWN YOU WOULDN'T TAKE ME UP TO FOREST HEIGHTS!
THERE'S ONLY ONE TAXI HEREABOUTS, MISS, AND THIS CAR WON'T MAKE IT UP THERE. THIS IS AS FAR AS I GO—YOU'LL HAVE TO WALK THE REST OF THE WAY.

So Tessa climbed up to the farm carrying her heavy case.
KATHY MIGHT HAVE COME TO MEET ME AT THE STATION. OH, DEAR, AND I'M SO HUNGRY!

Much later . . .
HELLO, TESSA, GOOD OF YOU TO COME BUT YOU'LL HAVE TO HURRY AND CHANGE—
HURRY! KATHY MUST BE JOKING!

I'VE TAKEN MUM'S TEA UP, TESSA. YOU CAN SEE HER AFTERWARDS. WE'VE TO GATHER THE SHEEP FOR DIPPING.
GATHER FOR...WHAT'S SHE TALKING ABOUT?
OH, KATHY, I COULDN'T POSSIBLY EAT THIS—POTATOES...

NONSENSE! YOU MUST EAT—IT WILL GIVE YOU ENERGY, AND YOU'LL NEED THAT HERE! HURRY UP!
MMM, NOTHING EVER TASTED AS GOOD AS THIS. I'VE EATEN SO MUCH I CAN HARDLY MOVE.

Tessa was kept busy all afternoon gathering in the sheep.
GOOD FOR TESSA. SHE'S MADE IT.
MY LEGS ARE SHAKING! I'VE CLIMBED FOR MILES.

THEY'LL STAY IN HERE UNTIL WE'VE HAD SUPPER. MUM WILL BE DYING FOR A CUPPA.
SUPPER? ALL I WANT TO DO IS SIT DOWN.

Later . . .
YOU'RE OVER-WORKING YOUR HELPER, KATHY. TESSA LOOKS ALL IN. I INSIST SHE GOES STRAIGHT TO BED.
OH, BUT I WAS GOING TO...YES YOU'RE RIGHT, MUM. COME ON, TESSA.

While Tessa got ready for bed . . .
HERE'S SOME SANDWICHES AND A GLASS OF MILK. TAKE THEM UP WITH YOU, TESSA—
OK, KATHY, YOU MUST BE TIRED TOO... AND I SHOULDN'T...WELL, THANKS.

Tessa thoroughly enjoyed her supper.
I'LL SOON BE TWENTY STONE BUT MMM, I'VE NEVER TASTED HAM SANDWICHES LIKE THESE. TOMORROW I'LL DIET—I PROMISE.
Meanwhile down in the kitchen . . .
WE'RE RUNNING OUT OF BREAD. THIS WILL BE FRESH FOR BREAKFAST.

Very early the next morning Kathy roused Tessa . . .
OH, I'M STIFF ALL OVER!
NEVER MIND. DIPPING SHEEP WILL SOON LOOSEN YOUR MUSCLES. I'VE GOT THE DIP TROUGH FILLED.

I'M PUSHING THEM IN THIS END, TESSA. WHEN THEY'VE SWUM TO YOU, HEAVE THEM OUT BY THEIR WOOL.
UGH! KICKING AND FLOUNDERING. THIS IS A MAN'S JOB!

OH, KATHY, HELP! I'M FALLING!
NO, YOU'RE FINE! I TOLD YOU THEY WERE HEAVY. YOU'LL HAVE TO DIG YOUR HEELS IN MORE.

And when the girls had finished.
COO! I'M GLAD THAT'S DONE! YOU ARE A SPORT, TESSA.
SPORT? I'M A USELESS, SHAPELESS LUMP COMPARED WITH YOU. BUT I'M GOING TO LEARN IF IT KILLS ME.

Back at the farmhouse Kathy made a huge pot of porridge.
THERE'S CREAM IN THE LARDER FOR THE PORRIDGE, TESSA.
GOSH! IF MUMMY COULD SEE WHAT I'M HAVING TO EAT SHE'D TURN PINK.

As the days passed by . . .
TESSA HAS A GO AT EVERYTHING—NO MATTER HOW HARD THE WORK. AND SHE'S LOOKING MUCH SLIMMER!
I'LL MISS YOU WHEN YOU GO, TESSA.
I'M NOT GOING UNTIL YOUR PARENTS ARE FIT TO WORK AGAIN—NO MATTER IF IT TAKES TO THE END OF THE HOLIDAYS.

It was six weeks before the "new" slim-line Tessa joined her mother at Gleaming Sands, and Kathy went with her.
MUMMY WILL HAVE THE SHOCK OF HER LIFE WHEN SHE SEES ME.
HI, MUM! WE'VE ARRIVED—
IT WAS VERY KIND OF HER TO INVITE ME FOR A HOLIDAY AS WELL!

WELCOME BACK, GIRLS! MY TESSA, YOUR FIGURE, IT'S GORGEOUS.
YES—AND I DIDN'T DIET TO GET IT!
IT WAS ALL THE HARD WORK TESSA PUT IN ON THE FARM AND THE OPEN AIR LIFE THAT BROUGHT HER WEIGHT DOWN, AUNT MAUD.

GOLLY—LOOK AT TESSA! WHAT A FIGURE!
HO-HO! THEY WON'T CALL ME FATTY AGAIN!
Tessa was delighted with her new found figure and thoroughly enjoyed her holiday at Gleaming Sands.

WILLA the WITCH
TWELVE-YEAR-OLD Willa Wichfield is a real live witch! Every hundred years, a witch is born into the Wichfield family, and the honour, or burden, has fallen on Willa.
One day, Willa shows a letter she's just received, to her friend Patsy Patience.
The letter is from the Grand Wizard of Great Britain.
IT SAYS I'VE BEEN CHOSEN TO REPRESENT ENGLAND AGAINST SCOTLAND IN A BROOMSTICK INTERNATIONAL AT STONEHENGE. I DON'T KNOW WHY HE'S PICKED ME, BUT I'D BETTER GO.
I'LL COME WITH YOU AND GIVE YOU SOME SUPPORT.
A few days later, Willa and Patsy arrived at Stonehenge for the International. Already there was Green Meg, the Scottish entrant.
I'LL SOON SHOW THIS WEE APPRENTICE WHAT A REAL WITCH CAN DO!
READY, STEADY...
Willa and Meg lined up tor the first contest which was a speed test. Willa's "broomstick" was an up-to-date model—a vacuum cleaner.
Off they went.
Willa forged ahead.
SNARL! FUME!
Suddenly Willa's vacuum cleaner back-fired and Meg was covered with dust.
Meg lost control of her broomstick and . . .
WHUMP

YE YOUNG WHIPPER-SNAPPER! YE DID THAT ON PURPOSE!
STONEHENGE
10
MILES

Willa was declared winner of the speed test.
HOORAY!

THE NEXT TEST IS AEROBATICS. YOU WILL GO FIRST THIS TIME, WILLA.

NOW I'LL GET MY OWN BACK ON THAT WEE HUSSY!

Willa put her vacuum cleaner through its paces. But Meg, out of sight of the judges, was up to mischief.
HEH! HEH!

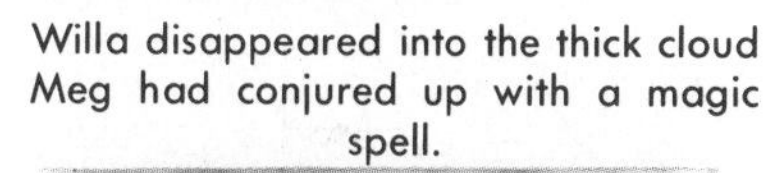
Willa disappeared into the thick cloud Meg had conjured up with a magic spell.

HEY! WHERE AM I?

Willa lost her sense of direction, and . . .
KERRASH!
CACKLE!

HEH! HEH! THAT'LL TEACH YOU!

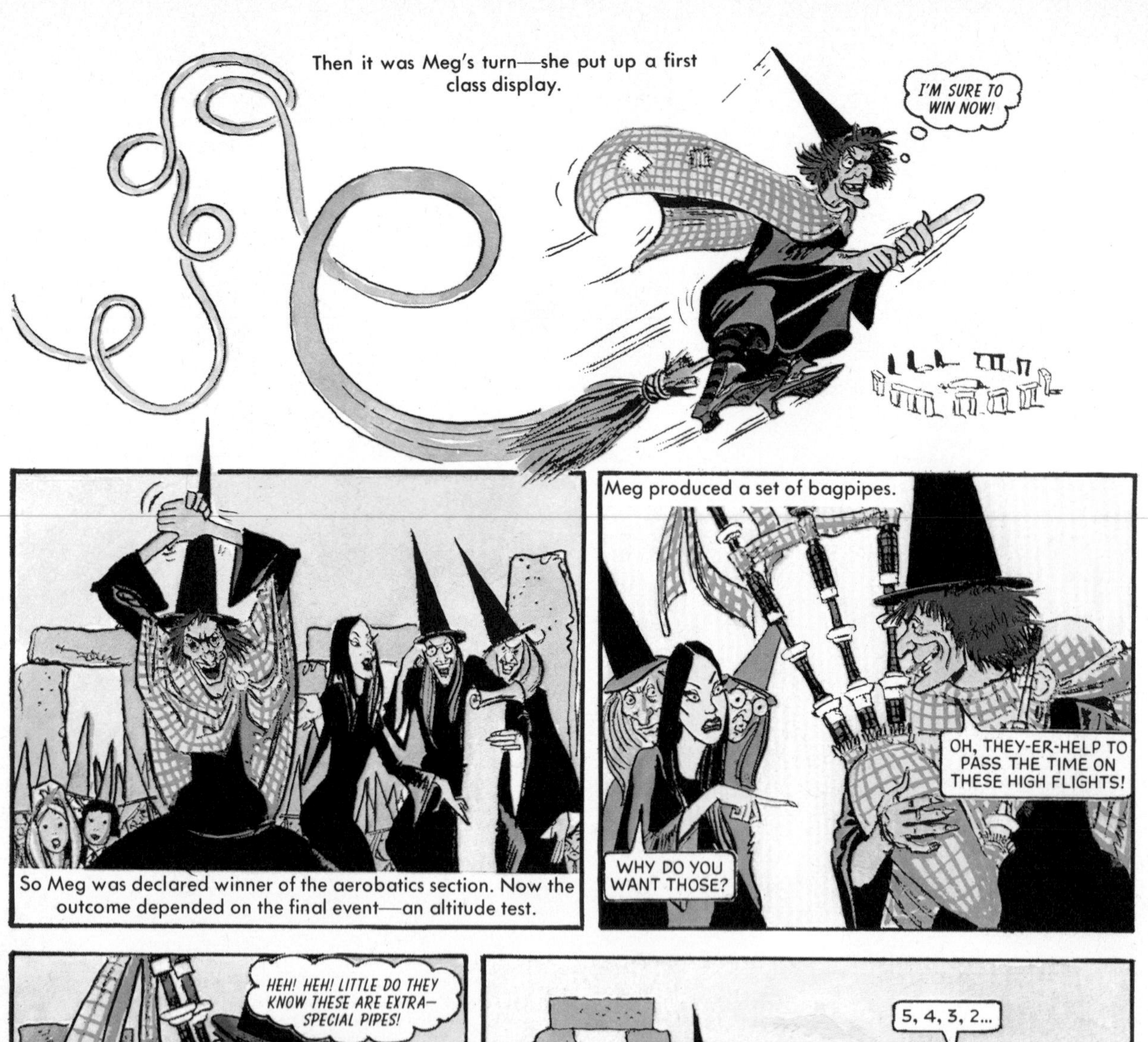
Then it was Meg's turn—she put up a first class display.
I'M SURE TO WIN NOW!
So Meg was declared winner of the aerobatics section. Now the outcome depended on the final event—an altitude test.
Meg produced a set of bagpipes.
WHY DO YOU WANT THOSE?
OH, THEY-ER-HELP TO PASS THE TIME ON THESE HIGH FLIGHTS!

HEH! HEH! LITTLE DO THEY KNOW THESE ARE EXTRA-SPECIAL PIPES!
5, 4, 3, 2...
WHEEEEEEEE
IT'S TOO EASY!
Meg's magic pipes rocketed her into the air.

MIGHTY ME! THERE GOES MY SPELL BOOK! NOW I DON'T KNOW HOW TO STOP THESE PIPES!
Spells
GOSH! I'LL NEVER REACH THAT HEIGHT!
Willa returned to the ground. Some time passed.
SINCE GREEN MEG HASN'T RETURNED WITHIN THE TIME LIMIT, WE DECLARE WILLA THE WINNER OF THE INTERNATIONAL TROPHY!
WHAT CAN HAVE HAPPENED TO MEG?
BEATS ME. SHE WAS LEADING BY A MILE, SO WHY HASN'T SHE COME BACK TO COLLECT HER PRIZE?

Much, much later, on the moon—
A THOUSAND CURSES ON THESE THINGS! A THOUSAND? TWO THOUSAND!
SAY! RECKON WE'VE FOUND SOME SORT OF MOON CREATURE, ELMER!

ROSIE RED RIDING HOOD

Later—
THAT ONE SURELY CAN'T BE REAL. ROSIE'S GRANNY WOULD FREEZE WITH ALL THAT SNOW ON HER.

Don't you ever learn, Wolfie?
AAGH! NOT AGAIN! MY HANDS ARE STINGING!

EE—OOH—AAH! PINS AND NEEDLES!
HO HO, WOLFIE! THIS TIME I USED A DUMMY TO MODEL MY SNOWMARM AND THERE MUST STILL BE PINS STICKING IN IT!

After Wolfie has bandaged his hands —er—paws . . .
HUH! SHE CAN MODEL HER SNOWMAN ON WHAT SHE LIKES—I'M GIVING UP KNOCKING THEM DOWN.
SLAM!

Suddenly—
SLITHER
'ICE'SAY! WHAT'S GOING ON?
SPALOSH

Just then, Rosie passes by.
WHY, I WONDER WHO MODELLED THAT SUPER SNOWMAN OF WOLFIE? IT WOULDN'T HAVE BEEN WOLFIE HIMSELF—HE'S TOO BUSY KNOCKING DOWN MY SNOWMEN TO HAVE—

—BUILT A SNOWMAN OF HIMSELF!

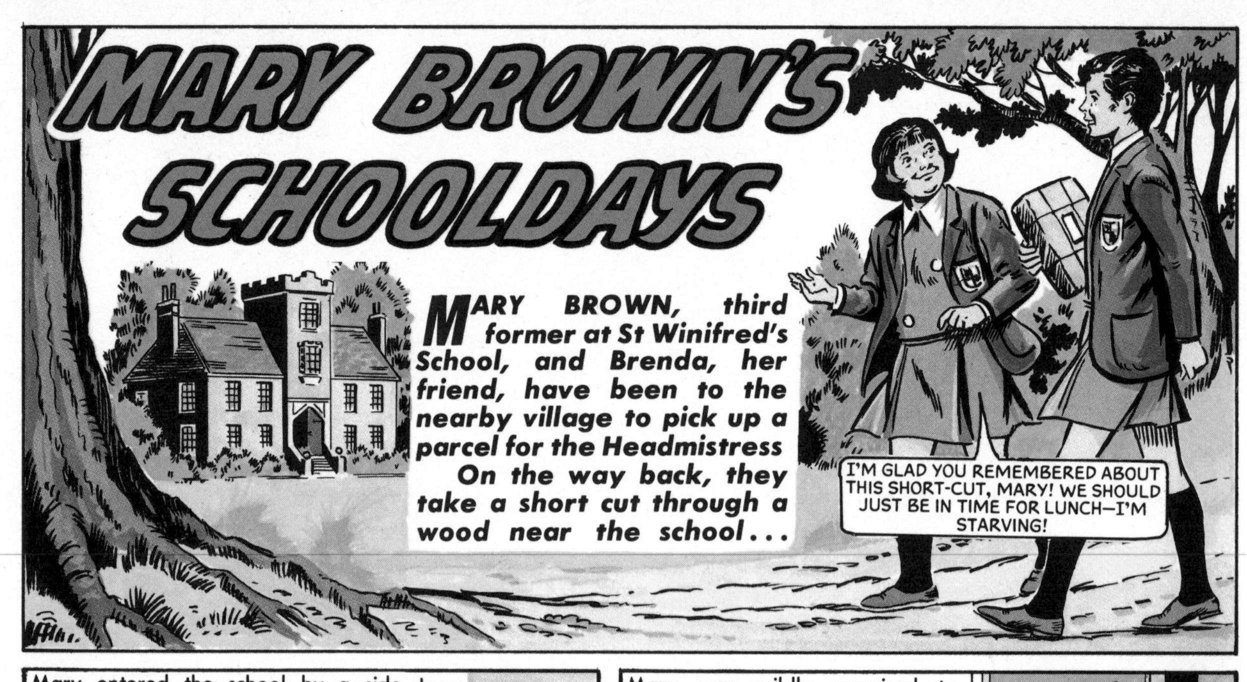
MARY BROWN'S SCHOOLDAYS
MARY BROWN, third former at St Winifred's School, and Brenda, her friend, have been to the nearby village to pick up a parcel for the Headmistress
On the way back, they take a short cut through a wood near the school...
I'M GLAD YOU REMEMBERED ABOUT THIS SHORT-CUT, MARY! WE SHOULD JUST BE IN TIME FOR LUNCH—I'M STARVING!

Mary entered the school by a side door.
I'LL TAKE THE PARCEL IN, BRENDA. YOU GO ON TO THE REFECTORY.
OK! I'LL KEEP A SEAT FOR YOU!
Mary was mildly surprised to find the door of the Headmistress's study open, and no-one inside.
I'LL JUST LEAVE THE PACKAGE. I DON'T WANT TO MISS LUNCH.
She hurried off to the refectory.
FUNNY! THERE'S USUALLY SOMEONE AROUND. THE PLACE LOOKS STRANGE.

Mary's footsteps echoed in the deserted corridors.
I'VE NEVER SEEN THE SCHOOL LIKE THIS. IT'S... IT'S A BIT SPOOKY!
Then—
MARY! MARY!
HEY! BRENDA! WHERE'S THE FIRE?
Brenda asked Mary to come and see the refectory . . .
TABLES SET, FOOD LAID OUT. BUT THERE'S NOT A SOUL IN THE PLACE!
WHAT ON EARTH'S GOING ON?
I MUST BE DREAMING! PINCH ME, BRENDA! BRENDA?
OH, BRENDA! HOW CAN YOU THINK OF FOOD AT A TIME LIKE THIS?

DO YOU THINK THEY'VE BEEN KIDNAPPED?
WHAT? THE WHOLE SCHOOL?
Suddenly—
THUD THUD THUD
WH-WHAT'S THAT?
SOUNDS LIKE SOMEONE WALKING ABOUT IN THE ROOM ABOVE.

COME ON! WE MUST FIND OUT WHO IT IS!
NO! NO! WHAT IF IT'S,A KIDNAPPER OR SOMETHING?
The girls crept silently upstairs.

OH, COME ON, BRENDA! WE'LL JUST TAKE A PEEK!

MUST HAVE BEEN THIS ROOM, I THINK!

Then—
AAH!
EEK!
Badly frightened, Mary and Brenda didn't wait to find out who the man was.
WHAT ON EARTH? COME BACK HERE!
RUN, BRENDA!
But—
STOP THEM, SERGEANT!
WHAT WERE YOU RUNNING AWAY FOR? I WASN'T GOING TO HURT YOU.
IT'S JUST THAT FINDING THE SCHOOL EMPTY, WE WERE A BIT FRIGHTENED—
YOU SHOULDN'T BE HERE AT ALL! THE WHOLE SCHOOL'S BEEN EVACUATED!
WHAT?
WE'RE BOMB DISPOSAL EXPERTS. ONE OF THE STAFF FOUND WHAT MAY BE AN UNEXPLODED BOMB LODGED IN THE ATTIC OF THIS BUILDING.

Mary and Brenda were taken to join the Headmistress and the rest of the school, at a farmhouse some distance away.
I SENT SOMEONE TO MEET YOU ON YOUR WAY BACK FROM THE VILLAGE.
I'M AFRAID WE TOOK A SHORT CUT THROUGH THE WOOD.
Some time passed, then one of the teachers came running up . . .
YOUNG BAINES OF THE FIRST FORM HAS DISAPPEARED. HER CLASSMATES SAY SHE'S GONE BACK TO THE SCHOOL TO GET SOME DOLL OR OTHER.
YOU STAY WITH YOUR OTHER PUPILS.
COME ON, BRENDA!
Further up the road–
WE'RE LOOKING FOR A SMALL GIRL.
NO ONE'S GOT PAST ME!
MAYBE SHE TRIED TO GO THROUGH THE WOOD LIKE WE DID.
THEN SHE'LL PROBABLY BE LOST!
I'LL CLIMB A TREE AND HAVE A LOOK AROUND.

From her vantage point Mary scanned the area.
SOMETHING MOVING OVER TO YOUR RIGHT, BRENDA!

OOH! A PHEASANT! WHAT A FRIGHT!

But then—
THERE SHE IS!

Molly Baines was only a few yards from the side-entrance to the school when Brenda caught up with her.
MY DOLLY—I'VE GOT TO SAVE IT—
YOU CAN'T GO IN, MOLLY—YOU'LL BE BLOWN TO PIECES IF THE BOMB GOES OFF!

But, when they arrived back at the farmhouse . . . it was completely deserted.
OH, NO! DON'T TELL ME THE WHOLE SCHOOL'S DISAPPEARED AGAIN!

But on the brow of the hill . . .
LOOK! THANK GOODNESS! THEY'RE ON THEIR WAY BACK TO THE SCHOOL. THE ALL-CLEAR MUST HAVE BEEN GIVEN—NO NEED TO CRY, MOLLY—YOUR DOLL IS QUITE SAFE AND SO IS ST. WIN'S!
The bomb which had fallen into the old wing of St Win's during the war was safely put out of action and soon everything was back to normal. But Mary and Brenda would never forget the day they were—the only girls at St Win's!

Hot JULY
brings thunder showers,
Apricots and
gilly flowers.
AUGUST-
brings the sheaves
of corn,
Then the harvest
home is borne.
Warm SEPTEMBER
brings the fruit,
Sportsmen then
begin to shoot.